Santa Rage

A Killer Claus Compendium

Edited by J. Alan Hartman

NAZCA PRESS

Sex can be the greatest pleasure or the deepest disappointment. It's an expression of love, a few moments of fun, the way to scratch an itch, a lifetime commitment, two (or more) bodies tangled in the dark. The human form coming together in perfect harmony, like musical instruments coming together to create the ultimate concert..

Twelve authors have penned tales of sex, crime, revenge, ego, espionage, and unexplainable events, each involving a musical instrument commonly found in an orchestra.

Couples, threesomes, group sex, same-sex, multiple partners, a bit of bondage, and one mermaid—no matter who they are or what configuration they choose to satisfy their lust, all participants soon learn, it's not just sex.

Of course, with just one wrong note…it's murder.

Paperback ISBN: 9781963479577 Ebook ISBN: 9781963479560

Santa Rage
A Killer Claus Compendium
Edited by J. Alan Hartman

Nazca Press is an imprint of Misti Media LLC and can be found at
https://mistimedia.com – and – https://whitecitypress.com

Contents

But First, a Word from the Editor…

I really wish I could take credit for the idea behind this anthology, but I simply can't.

Kevin Tipple is one very, very funny man with a dark sense of humor. He's served multiple terms as the President of the Short Mystery Fiction Society and the owner/operator of Kevin's Corner, a much-awarded website for book reviews. I've followed him for years and consider him a friend.

November 25th, 2018 is a day that will live in infamy. That's the day Kevin posted this to his Facebook page:

Been awhile since I have suggested an anthology idea, but this popped into my head from a post I made earlier. Anthology Title: SANTA RAGE: 24 TALES OF NOT SO JOLLY MURDER AND MAYHEM. *Based on the idea that one night, while out making deliveries, Santa snapped thanks to the holiday stress and went on a killing spree. Bonus points would be awarded for story elements involving meth or drug dealing, strippers, and the best dose of karma Santa ever dealt that did not involve coal.*

This post showed up again in his feed somewhere around November of 2023, where I saw it for the first time. I immediately reached out to Kevin and begged him to let me produce the anthology. He was floored at the idea of seeing it come to life and gave me his blessing. Thus, what might possibly be my favorite anthology I've ever put together is now in your hands.

The end result is definitely shorter than the original suggestion of 24 stories, but the tales go even bigger and bolder than I think Kevin had even imagined. From horror to crime to just absolute batshit grindhouse mayhem, this anthology is over the top in all the most delightful ways. If you ever needed something that wasn't such a holly, jolly Christmas I can promise you…this anthology is the antidote to perpetual cheeriness.

There's no doubt I'll be making this an annual anthology as it was way too much fun to put together and it introduced me to a slew of writers that were new to me and are absolutely brilliant. Huge props to all ten of them, including the aforementioned Mr. Tipple, for creating such utterly fun chaos.

Kill 'em, Santa. Kill every last one of those muthas.

Jay Hartman
CEO/Editor-in-Chief
White City Press
November, 2024

First Contact
Kevin R. Tipple

It was 2am, and the blood was still warm because the old AC in the Waffle House was barely working. It had been 112 just hours ago for the official high at the big airport and it was still 97 there this hour. My little part of NE Dallas always ran hotter year-round than DFW Airport, so I was pretty sure we might still be over 100. Summer in Texas, record heat and drought, sucks, and it was doing nothing to help my ever-present insomnia.

I'd always had it. But, after the kids moved out, and then a few months later my wife passed, it got way worse. I didn't want pills as they did not work and made things worse. Years earlier, I had an intense love affair with alcohol and it had helped some, but it also damn near destroyed my marriage. I was not a happy drunk. An ultimatum was laid down and thank god I had the good sense to stop. I also had the good sense that without her, if I started drinking again, I might never to stop.

So, on the nights it was really bad when I could not sleep and felt like I was coming out of my own skin, I got in my car and drove around a little while before going to the nearby Waffle House. I'd hang out awhile, eat, and surf on the iPad or bring a print book. This was one of those bad nights. I was a semi regular late-night denizen so my presence did not stir up the regulars or the two employees. Being the middle of the week meant it was also far safer than the Friday and Saturday night crowd, dominated by drunks, and folks who want to fight for no reason at all.

Jesse was on the grill, as usual, and had brought me a burger with everything on it and fries earlier which has vanished pretty fast. He was back trying to pick up Shelly, despite the fact that I was pretty sure she played for the other team. It wasn't ever going to happen. He was in the friend zone and would never get out.

The two regulars finished their meals and headed out into the night. A DPD car rolled through the nearby intersection with its flashers going and then they went dark. Anything to not stop for the red light that went far longer than it should. A typical Texas summertime night.

I shifted a little more in my usual back booth as the paltry AC wheezed above me spewing what it could to ease the temp downwards. I'd had enough of social media and got off in order to read the latest Terry Shames book. Texas author Bill Crider had Sheriff Dan Rhodes. Shames had Sheriff Samuel Craddock. Both had gotten me through many a dark period. Craddock was out talking a case over with his cows. As usual, they seemed far more interested in eating than helping. It came to mind that maybe I needed some cows to talk to when things were working me over. I doubted that my northeast Dallas neighbors would be too happy with that idea.

As I always did, I was sitting facing the door when he

walked into the place. Dressed all in black, the man had black sunglasses on over his eyes too. Dressed in a black t-shirt, black pants, and black boots was one thing, but the accompanying black jacket seemed totally ridiculous in this heat. I could barely stand the heat and humidity and I was in a t-shirt and jeans.

Not that I had much time to think about any of it as this guy, who looked like something out of Hollywood casting for a tough guy in a direct to digital release movie, came straight at me. At a little after 2 A.M. in the morning, with the searing drought in full effect and that had meant 70 something plus days in a row with no rain at all, he looked like he was here to rob the place.

Or kill me.

I'd been out along time and in recent months I hadn't much cared if something happened. Now that I was facing this guy, I wished I had not left my gun out in the glove compartment of my wife's car. Fat lot good it was doing me there. Getting old and sloppy was not a good policy for living long and prospering.

Without looking at them, he said something to Shelly and Jesse as he moved by the long counter towards me. I then thought that maybe he was actually headed for the bathroom which was just behind me. He would not have been the first to come in hard like he had and go straight to the bathroom. Instead, without asking, he slid into my booth and sat staring at me.

Well, this was weird. Not fake weird like some tuff in the news in recent months, but, in your face, direct threat weird.

"Good morning, Mike."

"Can I help you.?"

Jesse and Shelly were silent and staring at us. An overhead light made that noise they do when the bulb is starting to go out. The AC had gone silent which made me wonder if the damn thing had finally died.

"Do you suppose I could get a black coffee?"

His voice was weird too. Had a sort of robotic monotone lilt to it. I thought of the legendry movie series that had been ruined by the remakes and figured if he had been sent back into time to kill me, I would have been dead already. These things never seemed to give a warning in the movies.

"I'm sure you can."

I nodded to Shelly who grabbed the pot, a white mug from the small rack next to the pot, and headed over. She was white in the face and visibly shaking. I hoped she did not drop the pot as there would be a mess and hell to pay.

"Tell Jesse to put his phone back in his apron pocket, Mike. No harm is going to come to anyone. We don't need company."

I looked over at Jesse to see him hit something on his phone and slowly slide it back to his apron pocket. He stood, feet spread, and arms crossed like he did last spring when the kid came in hopped up on stupidity and god knows what else and tried to rob the place. Came in with a water gun that looked all too real. Hell of a way to raise money to take some girl to the Prom. This was a different deal, by far, and I hoped Jesse would not do anything stupid.

Shelly stepped up to us and barely got the mug safely

down on the table. It landed on the surface with a bit of a clatter and made my nerves jump. You could see the half full pot of coffee sloshing in the thing she was shaking so bad. I wasn't sure she could fill the mug at all the way things looked.

He took off his glasses and looked up at her.

"Stop. Look at me."

After what seemed like forever, she finally looked at him. Her hands steadied and then a little color came back into her face.

"Nothing is going to happen to anyone. I just need to talk to Mike. Relax." His odd voice deepened a little as he said, "In a couple of hours when your shift is over, you will be home to your little girl. Everything will be fine. You are a great Mom."

Little girl?

I had no idea.

"Thank you," she said as she poured the coffee without spilling a drop. Finished, she walked away and went behind the counter, putting the pot back where it belonged. Jesse was clearly shocked as he said something to her. She shook her head in refusal, making her long dark hair sway, and then moved away from him. About two feet or so away from him, she stood, hands on gripping the counter edge behind her, and watched us.

"Okay. You know how to make an entrance. You've had some fun. Fine and dandy." I shifted in my seat wishing this guy would just spit out what his problem with me was. "Let's get on with it."

He nodded like he was somebody in royalty dealing with a supplicant.

"What's your name?"

"That's immaterial, Mike." You don't need to know it."

"Maybe, Maybe not. But, be courteous and indulge me."

He reached into the inside of his jacket and I thought that maybe he was going to pull out a gun or something. With his hand still hidden, he sat there and smirked, as all the lights outside on the building and parking lot went off. As soon as they were off, the inside lights lowered to the dim low light level they used to have when the place was closed during the pandemic lockdown.

"That's better," he said as he pulled him hand free.

A DPD patrol car cruised by as did a succession of pickup trucks and 18 wheelers. No doubt the long-haul truckers were headed to nearby I635 and out of town. Nobody stopped to see why the place was closed or why four people were hanging out inside staring at each other.

I'd seen some weird stuff over the years working the nightshift. But, nothing like this. I was so out of my depth; I had no idea what to do.

"I'm here, Mike, to talk to you about your future. Simply put, you can't kill Chris Collins."

My stomach clenched. There was no way he could have known.

"I'm not planning to."

My voice sounded off and he just sat there staring at me. His dark eyes seemed to almost glow as he made no reaction at all.

"Yes, you are."

"No. Not at all."

Of course, I had thought about it a lot. It was all I thought about every day since he got out. I had the concept of a plan, but nothing to really act on. Yet.

"You have to know, Mike, that killing him won't bring Sarah back."

"I know!" I took a deep breath and said, "And while you are sitting here telling me things I already know, Captain Obvious, I know that there is no way a just and loving God would have put her through what he did before she died."

"Captain Obvious? Not bad." He snickered and then said, "I must say, Mike, you are entertaining."

"Look, the state says he did his time and justice was severed. I have to accept that."

"You haven't."

"Whether or not I have is none of your business."

"Not true. It is my business. You simply can't kill Chris Collins. The reasons why have nothing to do with faith, morality or anything other than the fact you have been told not to do it."

He took a sip of the coffee, made a face, and set the cup down. With the back of a hand, he slid it to one side before glancing at his watch. Like everything else on his body, it was black. It also seemed to shimmer on his wrist. At the time, I thought it was just a trick of the weird lighting. I also had noticed that he was not sweating though I certainly was as, with no ac running, the place was definitely heating up.

"Christmas is coming in a few weeks. Looking forward

to it?'

"Sure. Doesn't everybody?"

"You have to stop lying to me, Mike. You hate Christmas. Not just because Sarah died on Christmas Eve after you two had a fight, like some really bad Hollywood Hallmark movie, but because in the seven years since, you have not been able to get over her death. She loved Christmas and it hurts too much now."

I really wanted to jump up and punch this guy in the head.

His hands had been flat on the table as we talked and now the pointing finger on his right hand went up.

"Don't get up, Mike. You will not succeed in hitting me. The consequences for you trying would be very grave," he said in a voice that seemed to flow through me.

He shifted in his seat and the vinyl creaked with the movement.

"I'm pressed for time, so, as much as this has been fun, I'm going to cut to the chase. Besides," he said as he turned towards Jesse, "In about fifteen minutes ten guys are going to show up here drunk and looking for breakfast. Strippers and booze make a man hungry, Jesse. Get ready to work."

He turned back to me and then shifted forward putting his now clasped hands on the table in front of us.

"Remember the deal that Santa knows if you have been naughty or nice?"

What in the hell?

I nodded slowly.

"Well, he still knows. Granted, he had to sell the

company lock stock and barrel to Amazon after he lost it in Prague last Christmas and killed all those people, allegedly."

"That was real?"

"Very much so."

I remembered the video that had lit the internet on fire. What appeared to be Santa, or somebody dressed like Santa, had stepped out of what looked like a sleigh being pulled by ten reindeer. It looked like it was outside of some church. He yelled something and then pulled out some sort of assault weapon out of a red sack. He started spraying bullets everywhere as folks fled, if they could, or dropped dead where they stood. He then started towards the church, stepping over bodies on the way, and pulled something from his belt. There was a toss and then a massive explosion hit the church. He turned and opened fire again and the cell phone jerked and then went down on the ground wiping out the camera angle."

'That was fake. I saw the news stories."

"Come on, Mike. That is what they wanted you to believe. He had dirt on everybody who mattered so they released the story that it was an AI prank deal and the media ran with it."

"But, what about the bodies?"

"It was Prague, it was handled. Nobody that mattered, cared. Or, if they did, they knew not to care too much."

"Old man Claus still knew everything. Amazon put his stupid son, Billy, in charge, but he is just a figurehead. Santa still calls the shots and still has access to the database and all the surveillance stuff. Now he just sits on some undisclosed tropical island. On occasion, as part of his deal, he helps out law enforcement with tips and operations.

Sometimes, when somebody pops up in his system, he does some poking, and evaluates whether or not to intervene before they do something stupid and life altering. You came up, Mike. As one of the Big Guy's operatives, I was assigned to confirm the intel and intervene. Which is why *I* am here. You are not to kill, or cause any harm, to Chris Collins. Understood?"

"So, you are an Elf?"

I snickered and he did not find that funny at all. He just silently stared at me, and I was reminded of the look Dad gave me when I was a kid and he did not find me half as funny as I thought I was.

"No. I am what we call a "Tactical Assessment Operator" or TAO for short.

"You need a far better acronym."

"You are making plans to kill Chris Collins. That stops now. Persist and there will be seriously grave consequences for you."

Well, it was true. I was trying to figure out how to do it and how to get away with it. Hiring a hitman, hit person, hit whatever, was out as I didn't know anyone. I also didn't know anyone who might be tapped into that sort of thing or how the "Dark Web" worked where anyone could arrange for anything. I knew enough that I knew I had to do it myself. I just wasn't sure how to do it. I definitely wanted to get away with it as this guy was not built for the Texas prison system.

He sat back and waited for me to say something. A car screeched by as somebody decided they needed less rubber on their tires, for whatever reason.

"I sense a reluctance on your part to say anything. I'm not wired. I am not a cop or an informant. Stop watching so many police shows."

He glanced at his watch again and then looked at me. His eyes still had a weird glow to them in the low light, but the glow seemed brighter now.

"I'm authorized to tell you that Chris Collins will be off the board by the end of the year. You are to do nothing. He's been naughty….extremely naughty….and is going to suffer life altering consequences before the end of the year. Interfere with that, and you too will suffer significant consequences."

He continued to stare at me and seemingly, somehow, his eyes got brighter. I felt something I could not explain move within me. I then felt compelled to answer the unspoken question.

"Understood."

He picked up his glasses, slipped them back on, and slid back out of the booth. He stood above me staring down as I sat there knowing that if I did anything to cross him, it would be very bad.

"Remember that."

After I nodded, he turned and started back towards the front door. He got a few steps away, about even with them as Jesse and Shelly stood behind the long counter staring at him.

"I have been around a very long time and tasted a lot of coffee. A lot of really bad coffee. I suspect that cup you served me was the worst I ever tasted. *Be better.*"

He stared at them both for a few more seconds and then went to door. He started to push it open, and then stepped back, and turned to face us.

"Almost forgot."

He reached inside his jacket and then the outside lights powered up instantly. None of the normal minute or two warm up like they normally did, but just full on and bright. The inside lights kicked on as did the AC which felt better than it had. I also realized that the noise it normally made was not happening as the cool air gushed into the place.

"Your customers will arrive in two minutes, Jesse. As a football fan, you should get the fact that this is your two-minute warning. Sorry about the Cowboys, but your owner is an egotistical idiot."

He pushed open the door and then said, "By the way, Rhonda cheated on you. Get a paternity test."

"*Seriously?* You have a girlfriend and you are *hitting on me?*"

Oh, that did it. Shelly would talk about this for days. "Dude...."

Jesse rocked back against the stainless-steel prep table as the man in black walk outside. I thought he would still be visible as the door swung shut, but he was just gone. I could see the bushes out front and the base of the flag pole through the windows and the door, but he was just gone.

I looked at my watch and it was exactly four am. *How*

did that happen?

I was lost in my thoughts trying to figure out how what had seemed like a few minutes had somehow wiped over an hour and a half off the clock when headlights blazed across the side windows getting my attention. I watched as three cars came speeding in and parked. I found myself counting as one by one, as guys poured out of the various cars.

There were ten.

I decided right then and there to take the man at his word. All my life, I had believed that there are inexplicable forces at work that we did not fully understand. Or maybe, not understood at all. But, it seemed pretty clear that it would be best to do as I was told as I had long ago when Dad was supremely pissed and made it clear never to do whatever it was again.

I got confirmation on Christmas Eve, just before midnight, when Chris Collins drove his Chevy truck into a bridge abutment on US 75 going over 100. Nobody else was injured in the single vehicle crash. The resulting fireball was seen all over North Dallas and the surrounding area as was the fire that burned for several hours despite efforts by firefighters from Dallas and Richardson. Social media was full of videos of the burning wreckage for days afterwards.

Little noticed was the announcement later from the city and TxDot that the bridge abutment and roadway was fine and showed no damage from the impact of hours of burning flames.

The Anti-Santa
Alexander Bayliss

Twas the night before Christmas,
And all through the house
Not a creature was stirring,
Not even a—

Mouse lay staring at the insides of her eyelids. She never could sleep on Christmas Eve. It used to be because she was waiting for Santa. Now she knew Santa Claus was nothing but a pile of shit, a boogeyman used by your parents to bribe you and scare you and guilt-trip you into behaving yourself. Like her parents had any right to guilt-trip her into anything. Fucking hypocrites.

Her dad was out of town again, in Paris or Pensacola or wherever. Tomorrow he'd video call her from a hotel room, wishing her a happy Christmas, looking distracted, slurring his words, cutting across himself with a "Hey, cut it out, honey, I'm trying to talk to my daughter."

And as for her mother… Mouse got out of bed, crossed the hallway, and looked in through her mom's open bedroom door. She was lying on top of the bedclothes in knickers and a cami top, mussed-up red hair covering her face. On the nightstand were an empty champagne glass and a strip of tablets: She'd been drinking on top of her sleeping pills again. She wouldn't wake up until mid-afternoon. She'd be pale, panda-eyed, and full of apologies, right up until the first drink hit her.

Mouse went back into her own room and looked out of the window. No reindeer in the sky. Just low white cloud tinged orange by the streetlights. Snow swirling down. Two men walking along the street, stopping at the end of the driveway, and turning towards the house.

* * *

Mike and Yohan stood looking at the last house on the left.

"Time for one more," Mike said.

"I don't know." Yohan's voice was uneasy. "Haven't we got enough already? Maybe we should head back, grab a beer, get some sleep?"

"Bullshit," Mike said. "This is the biggest house on the street. Rich pickings."

"The biggest house will have the best alarm."

"Bullshit. A hundred bucks says the alarm isn't even switched on."

Yohan shrugged. "I'd take that bet."

"So let's find out." Mike tramped up the driveway, steel toe capped boots crunching through the snow. He passed a tool shed. Its roof was blanketed white. Outside the house were a Mercedes, a cheap Toyota, and a motorbike, all covered in snow.

The front door was hung with a Christmas wreath, an exuberant ring of foliage draped in red and gold ribbons and studded with bells, baubles, and pomegranates. Mike reached into his bag, took out a crowbar, and forced it into the crack in the door. Wood splintered round the lock, and the door swung open. Mike stepped into a hallway and shone a flashlight around. There was an alarm panel next to the door. It was switched off.

"Holy shit," Yohan said. "How did you know?"

"Simple—these folks are too rich to care. You see, the middle classes, the self-made men, they remember how hard it was to make their money, and they know just how easily they can lose it. They set their alarms. But *these* motherfuckers—they've forgotten what money even means. It's like taking candy from a baby."

"Taking candy from a baby is actually pretty hard. Getting away with it, anyway. Babies scream louder than any alarm."

"Razor blade through the throat," Mike said. "Job done." It was an off-hand remark, but its tone gave Yohan a sick chill.

"Let's get what we came for and get out of here," Yohan said.

Mike made a clucking noise, like a chicken, mocking Yohan's caution. Still clucking, he drew his pistol, a 50 caliber Desert Eagle, and stalked down the long, wood-panelled corridor ahead of them. Yohan followed, the sick feeling in his gut getting stronger. The walls of the corridor were hung with an ugly mixture of pictures: family portraits, modern art that looked like an infant's scribbles, a canvas resembling something a dog had thrown up.

At the end of the corridor, a heavy oak door opened into

a long reception room. Double-height ceiling. Wooden beams strung with tinsel. A Christmas tree that must have been fifteen feet high, festooned in twinkling lights. Beneath it, a pile of presents. On a coffee table by a fireplace, wrapping paper, rolls of tape, a pair of scissors, and empty wine bottles.

Mike eyed the pile of presents. "We just hit the fucking mother lode," he said.

Yohan picked up a parcel. Iphone 16 Pro. He recognised it without even unwrapping it. They'd taken four of them already tonight. Mike ripped open another couple of presents: a Tiffany bracelet and a Cartier watch.

"Sweet," he said, "twenty thousand, just there."

Yohan tore open another present. Some self-help book, Reinventing Your Life. "Piece of shit," he muttered, tossing it aside.

There were bottles of perfume, more jewellery, and women's clothes—all designer stuff, but it would be harder to shift. They stuffed what they could into their bags, and Yohan said, "Right, let's go."

"Wait a second," Mike said, "There will be more jewellery upstairs. We can turn 20K into 100K in five minutes."

"That's not what we came for," Yohan said. "If we wake someone up, things could turn ugly."

"Nothing's going to happen, chicken shit."

Yohan swallowed. He wasn't so sure. Mike stamped up the stairs. His boots thumped. The stairs creaked. Yohan followed, a good few paces behind. At the top of the stairs, there was a wide wooden landing. The nearest door was open. Mike approached it and looked in. Yohan looked over his shoulder. On a queen-sized bed, a woman lay sleeping, wearing only her underwear, straggly hair covering her face. On the nightstand stood a champagne glass, a strip of pills, and a jewellery box, lid open, diamonds glistening. Mike walked up and tipped the entire contents of the box into his bag.

"I'm the anti-Santa," he said. "Taking away what you didn't earn and you don't deserve."

The woman didn't stir.

"Sleeping beauty," Mike leered.

"Comatose beauty, more like!" Yohan picked up one of the woman's wrists and let it flop back onto the bed. He laughed in relief. "You could start a motorbike in here and it wouldn't wake her."

Just as he finished speaking, there was a bang and a clatter from overhead. Something was thumping down through the walls of the house.

"What the fuck's that?" Yohan said.

"Nothing. Some bird or some shit."

"It didn't sound like a bird."

"You go take a look," Mike said, "while I turn over the rest of the bedrooms."

* * *

Yohan crept down the stairs, beads of cold sweat forming on his forehead. At the bottom of the stairs, he entered the reception room, where he could hear bumps and grunts. In the twinkling lights of the Christmas tree, he saw a figure emerging from the fireplace—a stout man with a white beard and ruddy cheeks.

"Who…Who are you?" Yohan said.

"*Who are you?*" the figure boomed. "What a question? Have you been living under a stone your entire life? A fat man dressed in red comes down a chimney on Christmas eve and you ask *Who are you?* What kind of cretin are you?"

Yohan stood open-mouthed.

"Oh dear, looks like we are going to have a problem here. Well, let me fill in a few blanks for you. I am Santa Claus."

"Eh?"

"Also known as Father Christmas? Also known as St Nick?"

"But—but you're not real."

"Oh, so you swallowed the blue pill, eh? Santa Claus can't be real, because how could he deliver presents to two billion children in one night? Well, wait one frickin' minute. Because Jeff Bezos delivers 20,000 parcels a minute all around the world, and people believe in him. And Elon Musk gets upside half a billion people's heads, and people sure think he's real."

"How… How?"

"Oh, getting around two billion children isn't easy. And it sure doesn't make it any easier having to stop and deal with parasitic scum like you. Scum who defile the spirit of Christmas. And as the years go by, there are more and more of you *defilers*. It's becoming like a war. Anyway, let's not draw this out." He gave a thin smile, reached into the sack which was hanging over his shoulder, and tossed Yohan a small gift box. "Here's your present."

Yohan caught it, instinctively, but he said, "If you think I'm opening that, you must be smoking crack."

Santa shrugged. "Do what you like with it."

The gold wrapping paper gleamed hypnotically, and Yohan glanced down. Santa swung a punch. His huge fist caught Yohan under the chin and knocked him backwards through the air.

"This isn't just fat," Santa said. "There's a whole bunch of muscle under here."

Yohan landed across the room, and his head caught the fireplace with a sickening crack. He was dazed, head ringing. Santa followed up with a violent kick. His huge boot crumped into Yohan's groin, sending him sliding across the polished wooden floor. Then Mike swung the handle of his Desert Eagle down onto the back of Santa's head, bringing him crashing to the floor.

* * *

When Santa came round, he was taped to a chair. They'd used multiple rolls of Scotch tape, reinforced with thicker parcel tape, so he could barely move.

"So," Mike said. "Who are you?"

"I've already told your halfwit friend here: I'm Santa Claus."

"Bullshit." Mike rammed the barrel of his pistol into Santa's mouth. "Tell the truth, prick, or I pull the trigger."

Santa was trying to talk, but his words were an incomprehensible mumble.

"What?" Mike snapped. "Speak clearly, asshole, or I'll

blow your head off."

More mumbling. "Oh Jesus." Mike pulled the trigger, but the safety catch was on, and the gun didn't go off. Creasing up with laughter, he pulled the gun out of Santa's mouth.

"I already told you," Santa said, his face stern. "I'm Santa Claus."

"You're talking out of your ass." Mike picked up the scissors from the coffee table. "Tell the truth, or I start cutting."

"You want the truth? Well, I'll tell you the truth. The truth is, you're delaying Santa Claus on the most important night of the year, and this won't end well for you. I'll give you one more chance: Release me."

"Release me!" Mike laughed. "Not until you tell me the truth. Maybe not even then." He grabbed Santa's ear and started snipping it with the scissors. It was tough work. The scissors were made for wrapping paper, not human cartilage. He persevered though. Blood trickled out, becoming a river, becoming a slick, soaking Santa's beard and the white trim round his outfit. As Mike made his last cut, the ear fell away, slipping off Santa's shoulder and slapping onto the floor.

Santa's face was stony. "Ho, ho, ho," he said.

"Hard man, eh?" Mike snarled. "So maybe I can't hurt you. But I can hurt that sleeping beauty upstairs. I'm going to drag her down here by her ankles and carve her up with these scissors right in front of you. Let's see how you feel about that. eh?"

Santa's face cracked with concern. "No! Not that. Do whatever you want to me, but don't hurt anyone else."

Yohan saw a glint of triumph in Mike's eye. He had seen vulnerability, and now he would exploit it.

Mike tramped up the stairs, Yohan following close behind.

"Let's just get out of here," Yohan said.

"That fat fuck just beat you all around the room, and you want to bug out. What kind of cocksucker are you?"

"Okay. Okay. It's just giving me a really bad feeling."

"Shut your hole and grab her other leg." Mike had grabbed one of the woman's ankles, but she was a dead weight, and he was struggling to drag her off the bed.

"Uh. Jesus. Uh," the woman mumbled, before closing her eyes again.

Yohan took the woman's other ankle, but she kicked out, catching him a glancing blow in the eye socket. He reeled backwards. Downstairs, there was a roar like a motorbike starting up.

"What the fuck's that?" Mike said. He let go of the woman's leg, leaving her sprawled on the bed, and stamped down into the reception room. Yohan followed, hanging back, head spinning, a sick sense of dread rising in his stomach.

The fat man was gone. The tape had been cut away with the bloody scissors, which still lay nearby. Yohan looked over to the heavy oak door at the far end of the lounge, through which they had entered. It was closed now. The roar was coming from behind that door.

"He's getting away. Fat bastard!" Mike ran towards the door, pistol raised.

Yohan made the connection a moment too late. That roar was higher-pitched than a motorcycle engine. And the way it was revving reminded him of a-

"Mike, wait!"

Mike was a few feet from the door when a size 12 boot kicked it open. The solid oak door hit him like a truck, sending him stumbling backwards, nose broken. Santa stepped through, and swung the chainsaw down. The saw caught Mike on the top of the head and cut right down through his neck and into his chest. Blood spattered the walls, the floor, and the double-height ceiling. A fraction of a second later, the saw burst out through Mike's groin, and the two halves of his body slipped away in different directions, entrails and organs slopping onto the floor.

"Jesus H!" Yohan ran in the opposite direction. He launched himself at a window. The glass shattered, and he plunged through, landing head-first in a snow drift. Behind him, the revving was coming closer. The cold snow on his face helped him focus. Which way is the drive? That way, you fucking idiot! Go!

He got to his feet and ran down the side of the house, feet slipping and sliding in the snow. He made it out into the driveway. The sound of the chainsaw was receding. He ran past the cars and the motorbike, heart pounding, lungs burning. He was almost past the tool shed. Yes! He was going to get away. He might spend the rest of his life processing this shit, but he was going to live.

"Now!" the fat man shouted, and a girl stepped out from behind the tool shed and swung a shovel. Yohan ran right onto the blade, and it knocked him some twenty feet back up the driveway.

"Oh Jesus Christ. Oh no."

The end was even quicker for Yohan than it was for Mike. A single stroke of the chainsaw through the neck. Jugular veins sprayed blood all over the snow. Yohan's head rolled away, eyes blinking.

* * *

Santa gave a whistle, and his reindeer swept down from the rooftop, pulling his sleigh. Mouse stood staring, eyes wide, as the reindeer clattered down into the snowy driveway. They looked so fucking *real.* Their big, black eyes reflected the streetlights. Muscles rippled beneath dense fur. Vapor shot from their nostrils as they grunted and harrumphed, and a sour, musky smell hung around them. Behind them, the sleigh was huge and gold and glowed with a ghostly light.

Santa climbed onto the sleigh and took a small leather case from under the seat. He opened it, took out a bandage, and wrapped it around his head.

"There are ways of repairing this damage," he said, "but not here. I must return to the North Pole. Before I go, it just remains for me to thank you, Mouse. If you hadn't cut me free from that chair, this could have ended very differently."

Mouse wanted to reply, but words wouldn't come. Even thoughts wouldn't come.

"This must all be a lot for you to take in," Santa said. "Go inside. Get some sleep."

"I feel bad," Mouse said at last. "You see… I didn't… I didn't believe in you."

Santa's laugh was warm. "Understandable. Makes total sense. The arguments against me stack up pretty high. I mean sure, Jeff Bezos delivers 20,000 parcels a minute. But I'm just one man. And there are LOTS of children."

"So how do you do it?"

Santa waved his fingers in front of her eyes. "Magic!" He guffawed. "I shouldn't tease you. We use a time dilation machine. 364 days are compressed into one night. Then I get a day off, before it all starts again. I've said too much. But you did save my life, so I suppose I owe you a glimpse of the inner workings. Now, go back inside, get some sleep."

"But what about all this?" Mouse gestured around her at the body parts in the snow.

"Don't worry. We have a team of clean-up elves. By morning this will all be gone. Sometimes we go one better, and pin it on another defiler. Either way, you don't have to worry about it. By morning, your memory of tonight will be like your memory of a dream, or your memory of a random Tuesday afternoon 10 years ago. You might find you've forgotten it altogether. But if you do remember anything, don't tell anyone. You'll be committed. Now go back inside, Mouse."

Mouse thought about going back inside. She thought about tomorrow. She thought about her mother staggering about, trying to cook the turkey, burning her hand on the oven door, cussing and draining another bottle of wine. She thought about her dad on the end of that video call, dead-eyed and distant.

"So it ends here," she said.

"It ends here, Mouse. I have to go."

There had to be another way. "Take me with you," she said.

"No, no, no, no, and no."

"You could use a helper. There must be a hell of a lot of defilers out there. And I'm between jobs. And anyway, if I understood you right, it would just be for one night."

"Which is like 364 nights, Mouse. A night longer than you can possibly imagine. It's dangerous. And as jobs go, the pay is non-existent, and it wouldn't look great on your resume."

She shrugged. "I want to help."

Santa looked stern. "I can't allow any harm to come to you, Mouse."

"Who saved who tonight?"

"Oh, Jesus Christ." Santa extended a hand down to her from his sleigh. "What the hell."

Burn, Baby, Burn
KM Rockwood

"It's a special case." Mrs. Claus sat by the fire, needles clicking. She kept her eyes on the sock she was knitting, not looking at Santa.

Rubbing a hand against the tightness in his forehead, he stifled a sigh and took a sip of mulled cider.

They were *all* special cases.

Mail that came to the North Pole addressed to Santa went directly to the mailroom, where diligent elves read and sorted the letters.

But once in a while, a letter was addressed to Mrs. Claus. They were delivered to her, unopened.

Thank goodness it didn't occur to more people to address their mail to Mrs. Claus. She saw everyone as a "special case."

Now, just seventy-two hours before the big night, was not a good time for one of her projects.

But Santa knew better than to dismiss her concerns. She would never interfere with the preparations for the Christmas Eve flight, but he'd have to live with her afterwards. If he disappointed her, he could expect cold meals and a colder bed for days. Maybe weeks.

"What's special about it?" He tried to sound interested.

The clicking needles didn't pause, but Mrs. Claus looked up. "A young girl, Tangia, sent a letter for her older half-brother Maxwell."

Santa closed his eyes. Mrs. Claus was a total sucker for people who wrote in with a request for someone else. 'My sister wants a baby doll.' 'My dog needs a new bed.' Those requests, he could handle.

"And?" he prompted.

"Well, these two children were living with their mother. She died in an accident at work. Tangia's father lived there, too."

"Tragic." But surely Mrs. Claus didn't expect him to deliver a new mother for Christmas.

"Her dad took her to live with her grandma. Maxwell could have gone, too, even though he has a different father, but…"

"Yes?"

"Tangia—that's the girl's name—says Maxwell has *special needs*. He gets a disability stipend. Now he'll get some kind of payout from his mother's employer and great health insurance. His own father didn't want him until he realized that."

"Unfortunate. But perhaps his own father is the right person to decide what's best for him."

Santa was familiar with the concept of special needs children. An entire division of North Pole Enterprises, under the able direction of Senior Elf Henrik, was devoted to selecting gifts for these children, and modifying them when appropriate.

Mrs. Claus paused her knitting. "No. He just wants the money."

"Hmmm." This didn't sound good. But what did Mrs. Claus think Santa could do?

"Tangia says her brother's *neurodivergent.*"

"Ah." Santa was familiar with that concept, too. These children needed very special attention. Henrik researched each one carefully. He undoubtedly had a file on Maxwell and already knew what the boy would be getting for Christmas.

Her hands still, Mrs. Claus looked at him expectantly.

He stalled for time. "Isn't 'neurodivergent' kind of a big word for a little girl to use?"

"Tangia's a smart little girl." Mrs. Claus resumed her knitting. "She cares about her brother. The last she heard from him, he was crying and said he was being sent to a wilderness therapy program. Because of his behavior."

Santa frowned. "How old is he?" Of course neurodivergent children often presented behavioral issues. A wilderness therapy program, which usually took seriously misbehaving or delinquent teens, didn't sound like the right placement for a Maxwell. But what did he know? Maybe this was a specialized program.

"Thirteen." Mrs. Claus paused to slip the sock onto double-pointed needles so she could tackle the heel. "But Tangia says he acts much younger. She said he called her on his phone but while he was telling her about it, they took his phone away. She's really concerned."

"I can see where she might be." However, an important

component of wilderness therapy programs was to isolate the participant from outside influences. Santa couldn't say he thought that was a great idea, but it would explain taking the phone.

"She was hoping you could check in with him on your journey and see how he's doing."

Santa took a drink of his cider. The tightness in his forehead was turning into a dull ache. "I can't 'check in' with anyone on Christmas Eve! The flight is timed exactly so we can make all the stops we need to. Besides, thirteen is a bit old—unless there are younger children in the home, those kids are covered by an auxiliary flight, so I don't get to their homes myself at all."

"You'd think," Mrs. Claus's needles resumed their rhythmic clicking, "if it was an auxiliary flight, it'd be easier to fit something like this in."

"Modifying plans at this point would be a nightmare! We have less than three days…"

Mrs. Claus raised her eyebrows. "You always think you have to micromanage every detail. The elves can handle it."

This time, his sigh was audible.

"And," she said. "If you're getting one of your tension headaches, you shouldn't be drinking mulled cider."

Santa knew when he'd been beat. "I'll look into it, dear."

* * *

The next morning, Santa headed to Henrik's office. The sooner he found out what was planned for Maxwell's Christmas, the sooner he could assure Mrs. Claus that the situation was under control. Then there would be no reason for anyone to "check in" with Maxwell.

What was the point, anyhow? All children, even the older ones, should be sleeping when the present-laden sleigh arrived.

"Ah, yes." Henrik opened a folder. "Maxwell. Age thirteen. Right here."

He skimmed the papers. His pointed ears flattened against his head. "Unfortunate situation, this."

"How so?" Santa asked.

"Well, Maxwell is enrolled in a wilderness camp experience. That's when someone has behavior problems…"

"Yes. I know. The program aims to teach the child self-discipline and confidence."

Henrik frowned, but he nodded. "Right."

"What does Maxwell want for Christmas?"

"What he *wants* is a soft teddy bear to sleep with. And a phone to call his sister."

"Is he getting at least the teddy bear?" They got lots of requests for phones, but North Pole Enterprises didn't supply them. A teddy bear, however, should be no problem.

Henrik's ears drooped. "Not going to happen."

Mrs. Claus would not be happy, Santa thought. "How come?"

"This wilderness program—Changes for Second Chances—is kind of intense. Strict rules." He pulled a page out of the folder and showed it to Santa.

The page contained a picture of a big lodge in a mountainous wooded setting, along with a list of residents and the geographic coordinates.

Santa peered at it. He saw Maxwell's name. The coordinates placed it well away from any towns or other settlements.

"They confiscate any personal possessions when the kids arrive," Henrik continued. "If we gave him a phone—which we can't do—or even a teddy bear, they'd take it away from him."

"Really." Santa raised his eyebrows.

"Yes. They handle some hard-core cases. Remember that kid Belvedere?"

"The one who set his school on fire? On purpose?"

"Yep. Watched it burn to the ground."

Santa scowled. "Nobody was hurt, though."

"Just 'cause they all managed to get out in time."

"Do they hold personal possessions until someone is released and then return their stuff?"

Henrik flipped to another page. "No. They would just smash a phone. That's what happened to the one he had. Besides, there's no service. You'd need a satellite phone. We have a few of those, but we need them ourselves."

"How about a teddy bear?"

Henrik's ears twitched. "They'd probably throw a teddy bear into the campfire. In front of Maxwell. Better not give him anything like that in the first place."

"What will he get?"

"These kids are in our socks-and-sweaters program. A pair of heavy wool socks and a warm sweater. Drab colors, so it's not noticeable they have something new. Since the meals are a bit sparse, each one will get an orange, some nuts, and a candy cane. They'll eat that before the staff realizes they have it."

"What kind of Christmas presents are those?" Santa grumped.

"Practical ones. Best we can do." Henrik tapped his finger on Maxwell's file. "This camp, now, takes the 'wilderness' part seriously. The kids sleep in canvas tents. They really do need warm socks and sweaters."

"Canvas tents in the winter?"

"Remember," Henrik said, "these *aren't* innocent young children. They're teenagers. Most of them are on the naughty list. With stars. That's how they ended up in the wilderness camp in the first place."

Santa considered. "Is Maxwell on the naughty list?"

"No." Henrik closed the folder. "Behavior problems, yes. But we make allowances for his condition. He's a well-intentioned young man doing the best he can. Definitely on the nice list."

"Then why is he in that program?"

Henrik shrugged. "He *does* have behavior problems."

"Do *you* think this is a suitable setting for him?"

Henrik's ears trembled. "Not my place to have an opinion, Santa. The custodial adult makes the decision, and we work with that."

The mission of Santa, indeed the entire staff, was to provide what presents were appropriate for each recipient. Many, many children lived in less-than-ideal conditions. Certainly Santa couldn't involve himself in these matters.

Maxwell's father decided what was best for the boy, and the role of Henrik was to deal with that.

Mrs. Claus would *not* be happy.

Perhaps Santa would ask the elves on the auxiliary trip to peek in on a sleeping Maxwell. Then he could assure her that Maxwell was well and they had done what they could.

But when Santa thought about explaining to Mrs. Claus, his dull headache turned into a throbbing one. Poor Maxwell. The kid had enough problems without being stuck in a rigid wilderness camp with a bunch of delinquent teenagers.

* * *

Henrik was right. Where a child lived was not their business.

Still…

Santa's mind kept returning to the thought of a lonely, frightened, possibly hungry Maxwell wrapped in a sleeping bag, shivering in a canvas tent in frigid hills. Without even a snuggly teddy bear.

When Mrs. Claus inquired whether he had looked into Maxwell's situation, Santa almost snapped at her.

"Henrik takes care of that," Santa reminded her. "An auxiliary crew will visit him and the other boys. He's on the nice list. Henrik will make sure he gets suitable Christmas presents."

"Will he get a phone?"

Santa sighed. "You know we don't supply phones. And the program he's in thinks it's best if the participants are completely removed from outside influences."

"But if he could just call Tangia…" Mrs. Claus looked up from her knitting. "That would put *her* mind at ease."

"Well." Santa cleared his throat. "It's called *wilderness* for a reason. There's no cell phone reception. Or internet."

"How do they communicate with the world?" she asked.

"The kids? They don't. That's the whole point."

"How about the adults? Suppose there's an emergency? They have to be able to get in touch with somebody if a kid gets sick or hurt."

"Satellite phones."

Mrs. Claus started to say, "Do you think…?"

"No."

"Just for one call…"

"No." Santa tried to sound firm.

"But couldn't you ask Henrik…"

Santa rubbed his aching forehead. "I'm trying not to micromanage, dear."

That stopped her. She sniffed. "I will write back to Tangia and let her know that, although we can't put her in touch with her brother right now, Maxwell is doing well."

But Santa was pretty sure that in this particular program, young Maxwell was *not* doing well.

* * *

So soon before Christmas Eve, Santa didn't have time for Maxwell's dilemma, he told himself.

But that wasn't entirely true.

The elves handled everything. Competently. Maybe Mrs. Claus was right. He should back off and leave them to their jobs.

Glitches were bound to come up—they always did—but the elves handled them with aplomb. Everyone knew Santa should be well-rested for the big trip. It would take a total catastrophe before anyone bothered him.

In his office, he took a final glance at the naughty-and-nice lists and checked to make sure he knew where his hat was. One year, he remembered with chagrin, the takeoff was delayed because no one could find Santa's hat. It had been in the sleigh the whole time, and he was sitting on it.

Sighing at the memory, he got a mug of mulled cider and settled in his recliner for a nap.

But all he could think about was a lonely, frightened, cold, hungry, neurodivergent boy, definitely on the nice list, who had just lost his mother, and was now in an isolated setting, dumped in with older, delinquent boys. Bullies, probably.

Santa wasn't supposed to interfere, but he knew Mrs. Claus would never forgive him if he didn't at least check on the boy.

He'd never forgive himself.

Finally, he left his office, closing the door behind himself so everyone would think he was napping.

He went to the navigation/communication center. On Christmas Eve, it would be buzzing with activity. Now, it was empty and still.

Firing up one of the tracking systems, Santa fed in the coordinates for Changes for Second Chances main camp.

Way up in the mountains, truly isolated.

He slipped a hand-held navigator into his pocket. Then

he took one of the satellite phones. If anything went wrong, he'd need to be able to call for help.

But he hoped that didn't happen. He'd have a hard time explaining.

Maybe Maxwell could use the phone for that call to his sister.

Down by the reindeer barn, Santa looked for Astrid, the young elf who had just begun training as reindeer herder. She wouldn't realize just how out-of-bounds his request was.

Astrid was in the tack room, polishing harnesses.

Her ears perked up when she saw him.

"A small sleigh," he told her. "You have a training one, don't you? And a reindeer I can use?"

"Sure, Santa." She gave the bells a last swipe and put the harness down. "The training sleigh should work fine with a pair of reindeer."

"Good."

"Although…" Her ears drooped a bit. "It wouldn't be a good idea to take any of your regular reindeer out. We have them on a careful rest-feed-exercise regime to get them ready for the big trip."

"Of course. But are there reindeer I could use?"

"Mercury and Starlight are on back-up status. Just in case something happens to one of the main team. The back-ups haven't been needed for decades. You could use them. And Fleetfoot and Moonbeam are almost ready, too."

"Good, good. Can you harness them up for me—no bells, please—and pull the sleigh up behind the barn? I need a few things, but I'll be back."

"Behind the barn?" Astrid's ears quivered. "Is this trip a secret?"

"Well, I'd really appreciate it if you didn't mention it to anyone."

"Whatever you say, Santa." She busied herself collecting non-jingling harnesses as Santa hurried off to the warehouses.

What should he bring?

Food. He might need to win the cooperation of the boys at the camp. If they were hungry, offering food might help.

Or they just might mob him and take it.

No point in expecting the worst. Santa's entire career had been based on a fervent belief in the basic goodness of humanity. Especially children.

He passed over the groaning shelves of cookies and candy. From what Henrik said, they needed something more nourishing.

Trail mix. With yogurt-coated cashews and chocolate drops in addition to the usual dried fruit and peanuts. He grabbed a wagon and loaded it with five-pound sacks.

One more thing.

Santa headed to the overflowing toy bins and peered at the teddy bears.

Maxwell wanted one to sleep with, so it should be snuggly. And since Maxwell was thirteen, a big one.

He selected a soft, floppy bear, and added it to the wagon.

Slipping out the back door into the alley, he hurried toward the reindeer barn.

He hoped no one noticed him.

But even if they did, none of the elves would ever question what Santa was doing.

* * *

Clouds scuttled across the moon as the training sleigh whizzed through the night sky. A savage wind buffeted the small craft.

Santa kept an eye on the navigator as he zeroed in on the location he'd gleaned from Henrik's file.

He was accustomed to the smoothness of his usual, seasoned team. Mercury and Starlight were willing, and undoubtedly were doing their best, but the sleigh pitched and rolled as they skimmed over tall trees and skirted mountain peaks.

More clouds gathered as they reached the valley where the wilderness camp should be.

Santa leaned over to look for any trace of it.

The sleigh dipped sickeningly.

But there it was. A log hunting lodge with a snow-covered roof, its brightly-lit windows casting rectangles of light on the surrounding snow.

Smoke dribbled tentatively from the chimney, whisked away by the wind.

Henrik must be wrong about the canvas tents. A building this size might be hard to heat, and the kids might appreciate warm socks and sweaters, but it was sturdy and large enough to accommodate everyone.

No way could the inexperienced Mercury and Starlight land successfully on a rooftop. Even with Santa's steadying hand, they were likely to come in too high or too low. Maybe smash into a chimney. Possibly overshoot the roof entirely.

They'd have to land on the ground.

A ribbon of snow-covered but somewhat cleared road passed the building, ending in a clearing.

Santa guided the reindeer toward it.

As they swept down, a cloud blew over the moon.

They kept descending.

Just as they were within ten feet of the ground, moonlight lit the scene.

A gathering of small tan structures lay in the middle of the cleared strip.

The sleigh was about to land on top of them.

Santa shouted. The surprised reindeer pulled up, rising into the night.

He peered below. Could those be canvas tents? Was Henrik right?

Santa guided Mercury and Starlight in a big circle, they headed back to the clearing. This time, he eased them down and to a stop well before they reached the tents.

As the sleigh came to a standstill, a pinprick of light approached from the shadows. Followed by several bulky forms.

Teenage boys. Delinquent teenage boys. Gathering before him in an ominous semi-circle.

Icy fingers of wind crept down Santa's neck. He shivered.

Still children, Santa reminded himself. But he couldn't forget that most of them were on the naughty list. With stars next to their names.

He climbed out of the sleigh.

A hulking figure touched the pinprick of light to a twisted torch, which caught fire, and held it high to illuminate the surroundings. "What the hell do *you* want?"

"Belvedere!" one of the other boys objected. "That's *Santa Claus*."

"Oh yeah?" Belvedere took a menacing step closer. "What did you bring us, *Santa Claus*?"

"Trail mix."

"What?"

"Trail mix. The good kind. With chocolate candies."

No one moved.

"Enough for everybody," Santa added. "That is, if anybody's hungry?"

"For sure!" one of the boys called out.

"Let me get some." Santa retreated to the sleigh and began hauling out the big sacks. Each boy took one, including Belvedere.

Most of the boys opened their sacks right away and began shoveling trail mix into their mouths.

Belvedere stood clutching the torch in one hand and the sack in the other.

"I'm looking for Maxwell," Santa said.

Pausing with his hand halfway to his mouth, one boy said, "He's probably in the tent. He shares with Belvedere."

Santa winced at that idea. "Could I talk to him?"

Belvedere shifted his feet. "Maxwell don't talk much. He's kind of not all there, if you know what I mean."

"Not really," Santa said.

"Well." Belvedere looked beyond Santa toward the sleigh. "He's kind of shy. Scared, like. He don't come out of the tent unless he has to. And right now he's kind of sick."

"Oh?"

"But he'd like some trail mix, too. I'll give it to him."

Santa considered. Would the trail mix actually get to Maxwell if he gave it to Belvedere? "I'd rather give it to him myself." At least that way he could tell Mrs. Claus that he'd seen the boy.

Belvedere shrugged. "Suit yourself. Second tent from the end."

Grabbing a sack of trail mix, Santa headed for the tent.

Belvedere followed with the torch.

Santa ducked to enter. Inside the tent was no warmer than outside. No wonder Henrik planned to give the boys warm socks and sweaters.

A bundle lay on the floor, unmoving.

"Hey, kid." Belvedere stuck the torch into a holder made of rocks just outside the entrance. At least he didn't try to bring it into the tent. "Somebody here to see you."

A whimpering came from the bundle.

"It's okay." Belvedere looked over at Santa. "I won't let him hurt you. He got some food. You hungry?"

"No." The voice was weak and wavering.

Belvedere knelt down and reached a hand toward one end of the bundle, pushing the coverings aside. "Hey, fella, you're really sick. Burning up."

Santa leaned over and felt a feverish forehead. "This boy's sick!"

"No shit, Sherlock."

"*Really* sick. He needs a doctor. Where's the staff?"

Belvedere laughed. "You think they're gonna stay out on a night like this?"

"Where *are* they?"

"Two quit. Said it was too cold. Two took a few days off for Christmas. The others are up in the Commander's lodge. All warm and cozy."

"Why isn't everyone in the lodge?" Santa asked. "It looks big enough."

"Yeah, well, that's not the point, is it?" Belvedere shook his head. "Us kids, we got to tough it out in tents. Wilderness camp is about challenge! You don't give up just because it's uncomfortable. Or so they tell us."

"But Maxwell's sick! He could die out here."

"Maxwell needs to meet his challenge."

"That's not sensible," Santa insisted.

"Nobody said it's sensible." Belvedere tucked the coverings up closer against Maxwell. "Little buddy, you tell me when you want some of this trail mix. I bet it's good."

"Water," Maxwell said. "A drink of water."

"Sorry, kid. The water's all frozen. How about a little snow to melt in your mouth?" Belvedere backed out of the tent.

Santa scrambled after him. "This is outrageous. I'm going up to the lodge to tell them that Maxwell needs a doctor *immediately.*"

"The Commander'll love to hear that." Belvedere grinned. "The only way out of here now is snowmobile or helicopter. Nobody'll do anything until dawn. And prob'ly not then."

Santa straightened his shoulders. "They must be made to realize how serious this is."

Belvedere snorted as Santa headed up the trail.

At the front door, Santa lifted the heavy knocker and let it fall. No response. Maybe hard to hear with the wind howling. Needles of icy precipitation began to slash at the high windows, which spilled their rectangles of light onto the snow.

The door wouldn't budge, but locked houses were never a problem for Santa.

In the dim and musty hallway, he stopped to listen. No sound but the subtle crackling of a fire, which came from a room immediately to the left.

The scent of wood smoke mixed with an earthy, sweet odor.

Santa visited thousands of homes each year, and he recognized the smell.

Marijuana.

He tried never to pass judgement. And marijuana was now legal in places.

But that didn't mean this was a good idea for theoretically responsible adults, tasked with the care of troubled youth.

A task at which they seemed to be falling very short.

Most of those kids out in the freezing tents probably used drugs. Some of them might be here for no other reason.

These adults should set a better example.

Santa entered the room.

A fire burned low in the immense fireplace.

Four overstuffed leather chairs surrounded the hearth. Each held a slouched body draped with afghans and blankets.

As he watched, a man twitched, coughed, and settled down again without opening his eyes.

Santa walked farther into the room, his heavy boots loud on the floor.

No one stirred.

More afghans and blankets were strewn around. Bottles, some with their contents spilled out, lay on the floor. Bits of broken glass sparkled in the light of the flames.

The odor of marijuana was stronger here.

A half-full plastic bag sat on a coffee table beside a pack of rolling papers.

Next to that was a small mirror with a razor blade and a line of white powder.

What was going on here?

One of the men looked older than the others. Could this be the Commander?

Moving close, Santa reached out and shook his arm.

"Wha..?" he said, blinking. His eyes were bloodshot.

"Did you know that one of your charges is very ill?"

"My charges?" The man's eyes closed again. "I don't charge nothing. Pay cash."

Santa cleared his throat. "One of the young men you are responsible for."

"Hmmm…?"

"Wake up!" Santa shouted and stomped his foot.

Startled, everyone sat up.

"Santa Claus!" a woman murmured, her voice slurred.

The Commander, turning his head, said, "Santa Claus? I see him, too."

One of the other men chuckled. "Yeah. Prob'ly a figment of my imagination."

"Well, if he's a figment of your imagination, how come anybody else sees him?" the woman asked.

The man shrugged. "Prob'ly they don't. Prob'ly I'm imagining this whole conversation. I'm tired." He slouched down again and closed his eyes.

"Oh." the woman laid her head against the back of the chair and laughed. "Guess I'm just pretty high here."

The Commander nodded. "For sure. Flying."

"So Santa Claus isn't really here?"

"Nope. Hallucinating."

Within a minute everyone was still.

Totally unacceptable. Santa had to do something.

What?

The logs in the fireplace shifted. One snapped. An ember flew out onto the hearth, smoking.

The fireplace screen lay flat instead of being positioned properly, guarding the fire.

Jagged bits of firewood lay on the hearth. A box of kindling sat next to a stand with fireplace tools.

Santa frowned and reached for a poker to knock the ember back.

This could be dangerous. Suppose that ember had flown

all the way out to the hearth rug? Or landed on the dry kindling? It could set the place on fire. Those people, so high they couldn't keep their eyes open, might not be able to get out. An old log lodge like this could go up like a torch…

Yes, it could.

Santa stopped and peered at the sleeping forms.

They were obviously not responsible enough to run a wilderness program.

Look at the drugs. And the condition in which the boys were forced to live.

Was this an opportunity to put a stop to this nonsense?

Instead of edging the ember back into the fireplace, he pulled it forward, off the hearth and onto the rug.

He dropped some kindling on top of it.

For a few seconds, the little stack smoldered.

Then it burst into flame.

Santa tossed an afghan on top of it.

A smell of burning wool filled the air as it smoldered. Soon little flames broke through the fabric, making a hole and nibbling at the edges.

Santa turned toward the hallway.

He left the door to the room open.

He left the front door open, too.

A fire needed air.

Hurrying away from the lodge, he pulled the satellite phone from his coat pocket. When he reached the tents, he extended the antenna and punched in 911.

"Emergency dispatch," a disembodied voice said. "What is your emergency?"

Santa cleared his throat. "A fire."

"Structure fire? Wildfire?"

"Structure."

"Is everyone out of the structure?"

"No."

"Have everyone evacuate immediately."

Santa had no intention of doing that.

"What is your location?"

He recited the coordinates he'd used to find the place.

The voice was silent for a moment. "Is that a *residence*?"

"Kind of. It's Changes for Second Chances. A youth wilderness camp."

"And are the youth safe?"

"No. Some of them need medical attention. Right away."

"A response team is being dispatched immediately. It might be a while before they get there. Please stay on the line…"

But Santa punched the off button.

Mercury and Starlight were restlessly stamping their hooves, their noses lifted to sniff the smoke gathering in the air.

The boys left their tents and surrounded him.

"It may take a while." Santa lay a soothing hand on Mercury's neck. "But someone should be coming."

"Ah, the Commander'll just send them away," Belvedere said. "That's what always happens."

"Maybe not this time." Santa reached into the sleigh and lifted out the teddy bear. "Give this to Maxwell. And when they get here, make sure a medic takes a good look at him."

Belvedere took the teddy bear. "The Commander's gonna be mad."

"I doubt it." Santa handed Belvedere the satellite phone. "Give this to Maxwell, too. To call his sister."

"Can we call somebody, too?" one of the boys asked. "If we got somebody to call."

"Sure." Santa reached over and stroked Starlight's nose. "Just make sure Maxwell gets his turn."

"Look!" a boy shouted. "The lodge! It's on fire."

"Ohhh." Belvedere turned toward the growing glow, his face bursting into a grin. "I'm gonna get blamed for this, for sure. You guys'll have to swear I was with you when it started."

Santa climbed into the sleigh. They could make it back home in time for him to get a good nap. The fate of the missing satellite phone would have to remain a mystery. No one would be the wiser.

As Mercury and Starlight started to move, Santa glanced over at the boys.

Belvedere, his eyes glazed over, stared toward the flaming lodge. "Burn, baby, burn."

Whatever Happened to Christmas Magic?

Dante Bilec

Santa Claus hadn't scooped a quality toy off his assembly line since he lost Christmas Magic. Of every fuck-up that rolled off the conveyor belts since 1999, the *Marcela Muñeca* doll he held now took the Christmas fruit cake for the worst. It could have won an award for the toy that would most likely turn a kid into the next Ed Gein. If such an award ever existed. The doll had an ass where the face should have been and sparkling blue eyes stamped into the crotch area. Eye-testicles. Santa, or Zi Nicola as he preferred these days, avoided eye contact with the grotesque toy as he cast his menacing shadow over Candy the elf.

A freak odour of burnt coffee, ammonia, and stale sweat pervaded the control room to the machines running the doll assembly and overwhelmed Zi's nostrils. Candy's eyes welled with tears, but it likely had nothing to do with the smells. Meth cooked on a hotplate atop a table in the corner of the room. Clear hoses, beakers, and a distiller cluttered the space, along with a coffee maker irregularly blinking red light from its power button as it failed.

Franconetto, the head elf, followed behind the boss into

the room. He waddled in with his chest raised, but not beyond his gut or that nose which might have been considered an orator's nose or some shit like that in the old country. It was just an ugly beak in the new world.

"Who the fuck taught you to make toys, kid? Andrea Bocelli?" Zi asked, raining spit onto Candy's face.

"Ain't he the blind?" Franconetto asked, snorting. He poked a finger into his nose to loosen some snot or snow lodged up in there—a bad habit that worsened as the hair on his head migrated to his nostrils as he aged.

The boss glowered at the head elf barely suppressing the urge to smack him upside his coked-out head.

Smug expression melting off his face, the elf said, "Ehi, *cumpa*, relax." He spread his hands into a diffusing gesture. "I get it now." He always spoke as if he were a character in the *Sopranos*. Franconetto was from Montreal, and his father immigrated from Bolzano, which was practically the North Pole of Italy. Might as well have been Austrian, for Christ's sake.

"Look at this," Zi yelled, turning back to Candy. "You think little girls are gonna wanna play with a doll that looks like where you shit from?"

"I'm trying, Zi," Candy said. Blonde hair with purple streaks fell in matted curls from beneath her elf hat. The highlights matched the deep craters under her puffy eyes. "Jilly was supposed to be sorting mail while I looked after the doll machine." Unopened letters covered the surface of the control console. Some were stained brown underneath a paper plate with a half-eaten brownie on it. "She told me she was just going to get more coffee filters. That was five hours ago. I'll fix them all, I promise."

"Fix'em? You know how you're gonna fix'em?" He swiped the stale brownie off the plate and jammed it into Candy's mouth in one swift movement.

She whipped her head from left to right, trying to avoid it. Her screams muffled as the boss smeared chocolate on her lips and cheeks, and crumbs fell into her lap. When the brownie was all but crumbled, he pressed the doll's ass-face against her mouth, forcing Candy to kiss it as she slid from the chair to the floor.

"Ehi, Zi, don't you think you're being a bit harsh?" Franconetto asked. "She can't handle all that work by herself. Jilly should be kissing that ass."

"Oh, she's fired. In fact, I'm gonna wrap her up and stick her under the tree of the first little girl who had this doll on her Christmas list." He pulled the brown-smeared doll away from Candy's lips and held it up as if presenting it to executives of a toy company. "Don't it look better now? "No ass is complete without a turd between it." He threw the doll on the control console.

Mascara tears dripped down Candy's face faster than the solution from the condenser making meth chemicals. "I wanted this Christmas to be extra special. I let that kid down," she sobbed.

"What kid? What the hell are you talking about?" Zi slid a hand into his pocket and rummaged around. A finger poked through a hole in the side of his red pants before he pulled out a thin pack of Reindeer Reds and a Zippo displaying the silhouette of a naked woman in a Martini glass. "Actually, you know what? I don't got time for this." He put a cigarette between his lips, lit it, and started towards the door.

"Come on, Zi, have a heart." Franconetto helped Candy from the floor into her chair. "The girl's giving you her heart on a gold platter. You're supposed to be Santa Claus, the jolly guy, remember?"

Zi Nicola sighed, trying to expire his aggravation. "It was too long ago to remember." His shoulders relaxed. "Okay." The boss waded through the mail-strewn floor to the control console. He brushed letters from its surface and leaned against it. He gestured to Candy, inviting her to speak.

"When Jilly left and I started sorting the mail, I was trying to read some of the letters to help out more, you know, so you don't have to read as many last-minute lists before you go out tonight.

"We appreciate the extra help." Franconetto rested a hand on Candy's shoulder and shot Zi Nicola a wide-eyed glance. "Don't we, Zi?"

He nodded curtly.

"Glad I can help." Candy tightened into a slight smile through her sniffling. "Anyway, most letters I read were from kids asking for Marcela Muñeca, Legos or Nintendo, but this one kid asked for Christmas Magic. The weirdest thing, ain't it?"

As if they were two parts of the same toy, Zi's and Franconetto's eyelids peeled over.

"Did I say something wrong?" Candy asked.

Zi coughed. "No, nothing wrong. You were saying?"

"The kid made some good points and really caught me off guard." Candy tapped the left side of her chest. "Really hit me here, you know? I don't know how to give this kid Christmas Magic, but I figured making this the best damned Christmas since *A Charlie Brown Christmas* aired was as good a place as any to start."

"You, ah," Franconetto snorted. "Wouldn't still got that letter, would you?"

"'Course I do." Candy smiled wider. She undid the first button of her shirt and pulled a folded piece of paper from her cleavage.

Franconetto snatched it from her hands, the golden ticket to the magical Christmas they both longed for. His eyes darted back and forth across the page before he could fully unfold it. The elf's face paled, nearly blending with the white envelopes littering the floor.

"What is it?" Zi Nicola asked, taking a long stride towards Franconetto.

"The naughty list. I should'a known." He passed the letter to the boss. "This is our chance to make Christmas what it used to be." The elf cackled in a way Zi hadn't heard since that night in ninety-nine—the night they lost Christmas Magic. The elf scooped up two fistfuls of mail from the ground and threw them over his head. *"Just like the ones I used to know…"* he sang while doing a jig under the snowfall of letters. "Thank you, Candy." He planted a kiss on her lips. Seconds passed before Candy's face flushed to match her ruby lipstick.

Zi drew on his cigarette and read the letter as if the jackpot numbers were hidden on the page:

Dear Santa,

Whatever happened to Christmas Magic? No one cares about Christmas anymore. You can't even say Merry Christmas anymore. Kids at school say you're not real, but I know you're real. I bet the non-believers are on your naughty list with all the other bad people. It's their fault the Christmas Magic is gone. How can there be magic with so many naughty people sucking it away?

This year, I want the magic back in Christmas instead of presents. Can you please bring me Christmas Magic?

I'll leave you out some chicken noodle soup instead of cookies and milk because you're probably as sick over all this as I am.

Sincerely,

R.J.

"Cute kid, this R.J.," Zi Nicola said. "But I don't know why you're so happy. What does this letter gotta do with anything? I been wanting Christmas Magic back for years so we can maybe make good toys again and stop selling drugs to cover the cost of our dying operation. I don't know how to give this kid what he wants any more than I can give it to myself."

"Stop blowing smoke in your own face, Zi," Franconetto said. He plucked the half-smoked cigarette from Zi's mouth and puffed on it. "Come on. Think. You been so busy trying to keep up with the pressure of Christmas for the last two decades, and not that great, I might add, that you been letting everything go to shit—letting that naughty list pile up."

"*I* been letting Christmas go to shit?" Zi clenched his fists.

"Well, yeah. It ain't my job to sweep the naughty list. There's a balance to keep in this world, and Santa's responsible for it."

"Can you believe this fucking guy?" the boss asked, turning to Candy.

She shrugged with caution.

"Yeah, the naughty list is a bit dense, I admit." Zi Nicola raised his right hand as if under oath. "Shoot me for that. But if you wanna know where the magic went, look under Franconett's nose." Towering over the elf, Zi cuffed him on the cheek. "You got such big nostrils for such a tiny man."

Candy shifted in her seat uncomfortably.

"Oh, don't start with this again," the elf said, swatting the boss' hand from his cheek.

"Christmas going into Y2K Franconett' rides along in the sleigh to help me out. What a year that was. We did everything by hand in case all the computers and machines turned into *The Terminator.*"

"I think I got a Furby that year," Candy said.

"Popular toy back then." Zi Nicola nodded. "Anyway, we was all so tired from all the overtime, and *stunad'* the elf here thinks snorting a lil' snow is the answer. I fell asleep behind the reindeer reins while he did lines off the bottom of a *panettone.* I told him to put the shit away. Then what does he do? He rolls a twenty, shoves it up my nose and puts the snow through the funnel against my will."

"You didn't fight me much after that."

"By then, the damage was done. The sleigh went outta control with me trying to get away from the blow, and every single present in my sac fell out and went down random chimneys. Christmas Magic fell out with'em. That fucking year—when nine-year-olds got dildos, and lonely housewives got Furbys. Glad you at least got the Furby you asked for."

Candy folded her hands into her lap. "I asked for an Easy Bake Oven that year."

"'Course you did," Zi said, retrieving the doll from the console.

"Well, we ain't gonna find Christmas Magic sitting here chatting about it. We got work to do with that naughty list. I'll get my gun." Franconetto handed Candy the cigarette he had stolen.

"I don't smoke," she said.

"Figure it out." With a snort, he waddled to the door.

The elf's hope for Christmas Magic's return was as misplaced as the parts on the Marcela Muñeca doll. Beneath its innocent disguise was the reality of Christmas in the twenty-first century, which seethed into Zi Nicola's chest and added to the black iron weights that pulled him down further away from the throne of Christmas. He lowered his calloused hand on Franconetto's head, stopping him en route to the door.

Franconetto's eyes sagged. "Zi, come on. Don't be like

that."

The boss shook his head soberly. "Candy, don't worry about fixing anything," he said. "Amazon will get those dolls where they need to be."

Zi pushed past Franconetto and stepped out into the cold, damp air of another Christmas Eve in the twenty-first century.

* * *

Next to North Pole Toys' factory and warehouse, a neon sign alternated between two flashing images, giving the illusion of women dancing. Underneath them, the constant glow of red illuminated the words *Ho Ho Ho Gentleman's Club*. Where Zi Nicola floundered in the toy business, he also flourished in the trade of sex, snow, and every other street drug the mind could conjure. He even discovered a way to bring Quaaludes back from the dead with his very own special recipe. Customers looking for a fix never experienced a pleasure overload quite like that of his Nutella weed brownies. The only way to make them better was to find a way to package a complimentary blowjob with them.

Zi moped down the second-floor hallway to his office above the strip club. He would drink, he would snort, and he would brood. The only uncertainty was if he would finally make a long overdue decision about his continued involvement in the toy business. Before he could enter the office, his wife, Marie, bulldozed through the door into the hallway as if she were the Kool-Aid man. She clutched no fewer than fifteen overflowing manila folders against her novelty-sized chest. Ceiling-high stacks of file folders, not in the office the last time he snuck away for a line off one of his girls' asses, towered over her beyond the doorway. Zi could have mistaken them for the crowded teeth of some monster from a kid's nightmares. If only they had chomped Marie. But Zi knew better. He would be the only one chomped by those files.

Behind her, two ass-kisser elves, Joey and Sal, skirted around the file stacks to close in behind their mistress. Marie thought Zi didn't know about those elves. They *literally* took turns kissing her ass every night as if it were slathered in *brageole* gravy while the other trampolined from one of her tits to the other with his tongue out. He couldn't have cared less who kissed Marie's mountain of an ass or tickled her bean-bag chairs. The girls downstairs occupied Zi enough.

"What's all this?" Marie asked, launching the files.

Zi cringed. Marie's voice sounded as if it were produced within a throat lined with heavy grit sandpaper peppered with ground glass. "All that wasn't there this morning," he replied as the last few papers fluttered down. He fished a cigarette out of his pocket and lit it.

"Didn't I tell you to stop inhaling those chemicals? It's bad for you." Self-satisfied look on her face, she raised her chin. "I kicked the habit. I guess your willpower ain't as good as mine." With a hand held out to Sal, Marie snapped her sausage fingers.

From behind his ear, the elf produced a vaping pen and laid it in her palm.

"Yeah," Zi said as he walked past his wife, dragging on

his cigarette.

Marie followed with the product of her superior willpower held between her lips. She sucked back a puff of candy cane-flavoured vape. Poor Marie probably mistook the vaping pen for a real candy cane. Willpower doesn't always equal intelligence.

"I don't see you in weeks, and *yeah*, is all you got to say?"

"Yeah," he repeated. He entered the office. He didn't terribly mind the newly added stacks of files and papers creating a maze. They hid the peeling wallpaper, the warped wooden floors, and the grimy windows with frayed drapes. The light hanging over his cracked leather armchair flickered and gave him momentary glimpses of dust particles floating around him. He breathed deeply nonetheless. White particles from his years of snorting were bound to be mixed in by that point.

Weaving in and out of the paper columns, Zi approached his desk. It was wooden and mid-twentieth century but looked much older. Holding out an arm, he sent three specific paper towers, toppling over to reveal a painting of a picturesque Italian village hanging on the wall. The only text on the painting read *Romangno al Monte circa 1850*. Zi adjusted the painting. He plucked the burning ember from his cigarette and stashed the leftover in his beard to refry later.

Marie followed waving her finger. Joey and Sal weren't far behind. "You tell me you're way too busy with work to spend time with me, then I see all this." She gestured to the paper forest growing in the office.

Zi plopped into his office chair. It cried a sharp squeak as if crying under his weight. On the Sambuca-stained surface of his desk covered in cigarette butts and residual snow, a note from Franconetto suggested what direction to take with the files: *Give the naughty list another once over. –F.*

He crumpled the note.

"What've you been doing with all your time at work, Zi?" Marie carried on failing to notice—or care—about her husband ignoring her. "Fucking your whores from downstairs?"

Leaping out of his seat, Zi Nicola barred his teeth. "It's those whores that put food on the table to grow your ass wider and the dye in your hair to make it piss blonde."

Joey and Sal moved towards the boss, rolling up their sleeves.

"Oh please," Zi shouted. "Send those munchkins *affuncul'* before I stuff 'em and sell'em as Beanie Babies."

"They're elves, Zi."

"No, *I* got elves. *You* got lollipop kids. Now get 'em outta here."

She crossed her arms. "If they go, I go."

"Don't let the door smack your ass on the way out, sweetheart."

"You know what, fuck you, greasy wop. Good luck finding another Mrs. Claus." Marie stormed from the office with her elves behind her. A stack of files blew over in the gust when she slammed the door.

His girlfriend back in the day, Vittoria, was his choice for

Mrs. Claus. The white elves at the time thought Christmas was already ethnic enough since the old Santa chose an immigrant as his replacement when he decided to retire. Marie was their pick—the great white American hoe. If there was something *good* to say about the twenty-first century, it was that the era pissed on tradition. Hopefully, he could pick the next missus for himself—someone with coffee in her cream or, better yet, a broad who was full-on espresso.

Zi Nicola pulled the Marcela Muñeca doll out of his pocket and laid it on his desk. The whole lot of dolls was good for the garbage, but even garbage had its uses. He pushed the stiff button on his intercom. "Robbie, send Reyna up here."

While waiting, the muffled bass of the music below pounded his head. Zi pulled a bottle of *Sambuca Ramazzotti* out of his desk drawer and poured himself a glass. Before he could take the shot, a dainty knock sounded behind the door. "*Avanti,*" he said.

Reyna peeked her head around the door frame. "You wanted to see me?" Her eyebrows rose to her hairline at the sight of the paper towers in the office.

"Yeah, come in." His eyes never left her as she walked in. Reyna wore a yellow g-string-bra top combo that popped against her rich, golden-brown skin. She looked spent, no doubt from all the over-time Richie the Roman was making her put in. But even exhausted, the girl had the swagger of a geisha in stiletto heels.

"Is there something wrong with my work?" Reyna's

Filipina accent oddly caused Zi to crave a ripe mango from the Philippines. He could almost taste its sweetness, the feel of its flesh slipping and gushing between his fingers.

Breaking his gaze on her body to make eye contact sent withdrawal pangs creeping through his body. He cleared his throat. "Uh, the opposite, actually. You're doing so great that I need your help with something else."

Looking down, she brought a finger to her lips. "Really?" she asked giggling.

"Yeah, I want you to call Papi in Manila. Tell him to look out for these dolls with snow and meth crystals stuffed in'em when the next shipment of North American garbage gets delivered to the Filipino incinerators." Reyna shuffled back when Zi held the doll up.

"No problem," she said, avoiding a second look. "Papi will wire you the money when he gets them." Reyna hugged herself, rubbing her shoulders. "Don't you have to get ready to deliver presents? It's Christmas Eve."

The boss drained his glass of Sambuca in one gulp and clicked his tongue. "I ain't going."

"What do you mean you're not going?" She slammed her hands on the desk, tipping the bottle of Sambuca and him with it.

"Whoa, take it easy," he said, raising his hands, startled. "What's it to you anyway?"

"Christmas needs Santa. I believe in Christmas."

"That makes one of us." Once, there were twelve days of Christmas. These days, Santa couldn't even handle one. Zi guzzled Sambuca straight from the bottle. "All I'm good at these days is moving drugs and coming up with the next new and exciting way to get pervs into seats at the club. We had a full house for pregnant amputee night. Who would've thought?"

Reyna shook her head, disbelieving of the night's success herself.

"Ever since we lost the magic, I can't make toys right no more. What kinda Santa can't make toys?"

"Maybe I can help you with that," Reyna said, nibbling on her bottom lip.

Taking another swig of Sambuca, the boss hoisted himself out of his chair. He teetered in place momentarily before putting the bottle down and stumbling over to Reyna. "I appreciate it, but I'm sure Richie's waiting for you to get back on stage."

Her eyes darted to the door at the mention of Richie the Roman. "It's no problem, come with me," she said, leading him to his overused armchair.

Zi brushed against a stack of files and sent the paper column to join the Sambuca in pushing him off his balancing act and into his armchair. Following the tinny sound of worn springs, a dust cloud billowed around him when he landed. Reyna's lips spread into a smile that warmed him more than a lifetime of booze and drugs.

The worn leather of the armchair squeaked and swished as Zi let himself sink further into whatever stupor had taken hold of him. He would let Christmas come and go—all for a lap dance Reyna thought would help him reconsider. There were worse ways to trash a centuries-long tradition.

Reyna swayed to a forgotten record player in the office in search of mood music. Her rolling hips creating a soundless beat Zi felt in his chest.

He stopped her when she began to leaf through his records. "No music."

The swing of her hips dampened. She looked at Zi, tilting her head askance.

"Music makes it easy for you girls to hide how you really feel." Brushing his fingers through his tobacco-stained beard, Zi caught the half-smoked cigarette he had saved in the matted mess. He bounced the charred end against his belly, adding sooty stains to grease and armpit sweat on his wife-beater. "I like hearing you girls breathe when you dance." He lit the cigarette and took a long drag. "Think of it as the music of life."

Reyna's face wrinkled into a pout. The clack of her heels matched the beats of the boss' heart when she walked to within an arm's hair of him and danced. He stubbed his cigarette on the armrest of his chair, giving her his full attention.

Who was this girl? Sure, he was the boss, but the other girls would've at least swallowed hard at the idea of being sexy in front of a guy like him. An image of Reyna in an outfit from Mrs. Claus' wardrobe flashed in his mind. It kindled within him a feeling from a bygone era that hit faster than any heroin high.

Zi cupped his hands around Reyna's ass, which could likely deflect bullets. The startled squeal that came when he yanked her close fed that feeling cycling through him. He engulfed his face in her chest. All the while, he wound his thumbs around her g-string. A hand crawled up the dancer's backside and unlaced her top. Tits dropped out in relief. The last bit of her clothing restricted Zi's sensation of the dancer's heat radiating between her legs. Sliding to Reyna's front side along the material of her g-string, he tugged it down bit by bit, his hands moving with the motion of her hips.

With a rap that sent the door to his office swooshing open, Richie the Roman burst in, face redder than the blood in Zi's hard-on. "Where the fuck are you?" he called out. "Get out from behind the papers and get downstairs. The customers are getting tired of the fire bush on stage. The one-legged pregnant broad ain't here to cover. The customers want some Asian pussy in their faces."

Reyna wrapped her arms around herself and cowered under Richie's voice before Zi registered the intrusion. He brought a finger underneath her chin and diverted her back to him. Another woman looked back, corrupted by fear from the enduring rot of a demon's will continually forced on her. He scooted to the armchair's edge and heaved himself up with a grunt. Sucking in, he slipped around a paper stack with his chest puffed to meet Richie the Roman.

"Oh, sorry, Zi. I didn't know it was you who called her," Richie said, running a hand through his slick black hair. He was clean-shaven and smelled as if he had bathed in a cologne as expensive as his Roberto Cavalli suit.

"Yeah? Why else would she be here?"

Richie cleared his throat. "I dunno I thought you would

be getting ready for the big night. Not in here." He shifted in place, his forehead beginning to outshine his hair. "Anyway, I'll leave her to you. Sorry for the interruption." Inching towards the door, he raised his hand to wave.

"Wait, you can't go." Zi trapped Richie in a playful headlock and noogied him to his desk. "You gotta have a drink with me." He poured Sambuca into the only glass on the desk and handed it to Richie.

"What about you?" he asked, noting no other visible glasses.

"I'll drink from the bottle. *Salut'*." The boss clinked the bottle against Richie's glass and drained the remainder of the liquor faster than Richie could handle his shot. "Atta boy," he said when Richie finally flipped his empty glass onto the desk. "Good?"

"It's okay. I prefer cognac," he replied, failing to hide a grimace and all the malice of his being.

"Too fancy for me." With speed fueled by decades of suppressed rage, Zi shattered the empty bottle of Sambuca over Richie's head. As he collapsed to the floor, convulsing, the boss grabbed him behind the neck with a meaty smack and thrust the bottleneck of jagged glass that remained into Richie's jugular. By the second pulse of blood spurting, his eyes fluttered closed. The thought to say something clever like "Merry Christmas, ya filthy animal," blasted from Zi's mind before he could press his lips to utter the first syllable.

When Richie's face finally hit worn hardwood with a squelching thud, the column of papers next to Zi jumped amid a pop and a flash of light as if a firecracker exploded under it. The stack toppled over to join the mess on the floor, but not before a single manila folder landed in his hands. The boss flipped the file open to the naughty list's members having last names beginning in "R.O." Somewhere between Kimberly Robichaud and Tyler Roman, a name reading Ricardo Roma crossed away in red ink by an unseen pen, like magic—Christmas Magic.

That R.J. kid was right. Even Franconetto was right for once.

"Looks like you were on my shit list Ricardo Roma, or whatever the fuck your name is." Zi Nicola spat on Richie's corpse as it bled out.

Reyna sprinted into his arms, nearly sending him for a dip in blood. "Did he hurt you?"

"No. But I know he hurt you," he replied, caressing the back of her head. Zi led her to the record player and loaded it with his favourite album. "I think you're right," he said, moving cobwebs aside. "A little music wouldn't hurt."

As the first notes of Roy Orbison's "Pretty Paper" streamed from the speakers, Zi returned to his desk and paged Robbie on the intercom. "Get the sleigh ready, Robbie. Next to the sac, load all my weapons from the anti-narc cabinet with all the ammo. I'll need it."

"Aren't you going to stay and listen to music with me?" Reyna asked.

He stopped. "Reyna. Is that your real name?"

"Reyna-Janelle, but my friends call me R.J."

Shaking his head, Zi chuckled and let out a sigh. "R.J., I can't stay. I got work to do."

She nodded, understanding. "Happy holidays, big man."

"We both know *Merry Christmas* is better," he said, feeling more like Santa Claus again. "Thank you," he whispered under his breath. He felt the warmth of R.J.'s smile on his back as he left to prepare for a night with the added chore of the naughty list—the longest night of his career.

But then…Santa would have his first real Christmas of the 21st Century.

Magic and all.

Santa and Cinnamon
Kurtis Rupé

As I sit at my command post, watching chaos and destruction spread like wildfire across the globe, I can't help but feel a sense of resignation and exhaustion. Wars, disasters, inequality, and injustice—it's all a bunch of crap. My heart is sick with it, yet I can't help but feel I'm partly to blame. After all, I'm the one who's supposed to bring joy and happiness to children everywhere. But how can I do that when there's so much suffering and despair?

I rub my temples, trying to ease the tension in my head. I'm fed up with the whining, entitlement, and lack of gratitude from folks. They take and take without ever giving back. And I'm stuck in the middle, expected to deliver a never-ending supply of toys and cheer.

I released a disgusted sigh. What can I do to make a difference? These problems are so much bigger than me. I think about all the children who will be disappointed this year, all the families who will struggle to make ends meet, and the innocent people who will suffer because of the actions of others.

Then, Fen Thornfrost, one of the elves who always finds a creative way to bust my balls, walks in with a concerned look. "Hey, Santa, you okay? You look like you're about to implode."

I scowl, not in the mood. "I'm fine, Fen. Just peachy. The state of the world is just superb, and I'm thrilled to be a part of it."

Fen raises an eyebrow, unfazed by my sarcasm. "I think you just need to get your chimney swept, Santa," a reference to my unmet need for a romantic life, which he reminds me frequently is the source of my grouchiness. "But, if you're fine, maybe you can tell me why toy production is behind schedule. We need all hands on deck to meet the deadline."

I storm out of the room with a grunt of acknowledgment. Fucking elves. Lascivious and impish but charming, they are also warm and loyal friends, and Fen is one of my best. Truth is, he may be right. There is neither a Mrs. Claus nor a Mr. Claus. That whole Trad Wife thing was some bullshit created by corporate marketing people for the delicate sensibilities of the mid-Twentieth Century. Santa definitely gets a little lonely at the North Pole.

"Just to be clear," Fen called back to me from the room I had left, "I said 'all hands on deck,' not 'on dick.'"

Fucking elves.

* * *

In the dilapidated Belleview neighborhood, I ventured forth on my deliveries beneath a sky bruised with purple menace. The discordant sound of revelry hummed as the SantaCon bar crawl reached its crescendo. Not that I mind good-natured and friendly debauchery from time to time, but the sight that greeted me was disheartening—drunken impostors in my uniform out on the streets, belting out lewd songs and smashing bottles against sidewalks and walls.

My usual jovial countenance faltered at the sight of these miscreants mocking the spirit I'm entrusted to uphold. Each intoxicated laugh and shout screeched like a knife to my heart, tarnishing the festive cheer that should encompass this night.

The sight of hundreds of fake Santas staggering through the streets in shameless revelry spattered my joy like their remnants of puke in the brick-walled alley behind the Red Sled Strip Club. It left me questioning why I continued to wear this symbol of a season that seemed to have forgotten the essence of its true spirit.

* * *

Macon deGrump was the owner of the Red Sled Strip Club, which he used as a front for drug and sex trafficking, and was responsible for much of the decay in the Belleview neighborhood. Tonight, of all nights, he closed his club to the public. He was throwing a private holiday party for his employees: the soldiers, suppliers, associates, enforcers, bagmen, lieutenants, capos and associated hangers-on who facilitated his greasy hold on the neighborhood.

I followed some Santa imposters as they headed into the Red Sled Strip Club, the jingle of my bells contrasting with the raucous music inside. I straightened my red suit and took a long, deep breath, inhaling the humid funk of booze, sweat, and dirty money.

A group of three rowdy degenerates suddenly interrupted the dancers by climbing on stage with them in the middle of their routines. The dancers scattered like a covey of quail to the other side of the stage, where they gathered together. Their costumes shimmered under the swirling, multi-colored lights as the bouncers tossed the offenders back onto the floor.

Among the dancers, one stripper stood out with her shining box braids and a determined smile. She took charge, leading the others to return to the stage and regain the audience's attention.

I made my way through the crowd with determined strides. The patrons, many dressed in SantaCon attire, parted before me, their eyes wide with curiosity. I could hear their nervous whispers behind my ears. They may have thought I was just another employee or a paid performer, but the truth would soon become apparent.

I turned to make my way towards the stage, the scent of peppermint trailing in my wake. Cinnamon stood center stage, a scantily clad vision of caramel-skinned beauty. She froze mid-dance as I stepped into view, my tall figure looming at the foot of the platform. I offered her a playful wink, and she returned a hesitant smile.

With a flourish, I reached into my bag and produced the Nice List, its ancient parchment yellowed with age. I scanned the familiar names with a critical eye, lips pursed, before looking up at her, a twinkle in my eye. "You, my dear, are most certainly on the Nice List," I boomed, my voice carrying over loud music and the raucous partiers. With a grand gesture, I withdrew a gift from my sack, a rather long and brightly wrapped package tied with a satin bow, and presented it to her. "For the dancer who sets the night ablaze," I said.

Cinnamon, hesitant but curious, approached and carefully took the gift from my outstretched hand as a magical warmth spread through the air, tinged with the sweet scent of spice. The magical fabric shimmered, then dissolved to reveal a breathtaking sight.

It wasn't the traditional chrome or brass pole a dancer might expect. This one was crafted from a single, smooth piece of cinnamon wood, its surface polished to a mirror-like sheen. Delicate carvings of swirling snowflakes and dancing elves adorned its length, each glowing faintly with an ethereal light.

Cinnamon gasped, her eyes wide with wonder. This wasn't just a pole; it was a piece of magic, a celebration of her art intertwined with the spirit of Christmas. It was a gift befitting her talent and dedication. A slow smile spread across her face, replacing surprise with a newfound determination. "Santa," she whispered, her voice husky with emotion. "This is...incredible."

She continued in a voice a soft contrast to the blaring music. "I... I want to talk to you about Macon deGrump." Cinnamon's eyes, shimmering with unshed tears, betrayed the strength in her voice. "He's done terrible things, and I want... I need to make him pay." Her words hung there, each syllable laced with the weight of her painful past.

Leaning closer, I gently touched her, offering a reassuring smile. "Cinnamon, my dear, I understand your desire for retribution." I paused, choosing my words carefully, aware of the delicate nature of her request. "But tell me, what is it that you seek? What wrongs do you wish to right?"

Tears welled in Cinnamon's light brown eyes, but her choked voice held an unwavering resolve. "He... he forced himself on me, Santa," she whispered. "Made me feel like a cheap trick, a toy for his amusement. But that's not all." Her breath hitched, and she clutched the cinnamon pole tighter, knuckles white. "He threatened my daughter, Ava. She's only ten years old. He told me she'd be next if I didn't do what he wanted. One of his working girls strung out on meth and used up before she even had a chance at life." A sob escaped her lips, raw and desperate. "I can't let that happen, Santa. Not my Ava."

I listened, my heart heavy with the realization that Cinnamon, despite her captivating presence, was still a soul in need of solace. "Cinnamon," I began, my voice gentle but firm. "You are not alone in this quest. I will help you however I can. Together, we will show deGrump that no one, regardless of their power, is above the reach of justice."

"Now, my dear, I believe it's time for a little show," I said with a mischievous grin. "But first, I have a little surprise for the rest of this naughty lot."

Cinnamon smiled at me with grateful eyes. Then, as if she had read my mind, I watched her gather the other performers and lead them to the back exit for safety.

The air in Macon deGrump's club stank of something far worse than stale beer and desperation. It reeked of corruption. My boots thudded upon the grimy floor like the knell of funeral bells. Gone was jolly Santa, replaced by a harbinger of my cold vengeance.

The thumping pulse of the music sputtered and died. Faces, once masks of forced levity, contorted into raw terror. Macon deGrump, that greasy kingpin with a face like a melting snowman, cowered in a corner booth. His entourage of barely-legal women scattered, leaving him exposed – a shivering, yellow island in a sea of red velvet.

"Well, well, Macon," I snarled in a guttural rasp that sent chills down even the bouncers' spines. "Fancy seeing you on top of the naughty list this year. Again." The fear in his eyes, usually masked by a practiced leer, was naked and primal.

Beside him, Razor, his primary enforcer – a walking canvas of prison tattoos – shrank back like a cornered dog. His bravado, usually as thick as his neck, evaporated.

"S-Santa?" DeGrump stammered in a voice bordering on a squeak. "What brings you to...uh... my humble establishment?"

"Let's just say," I growled, letting each word drip with murderous intent, "Cinnamon has a friend at the North Pole. And harming a friend of Santa's gets you a one-way ticket to the express lane of naughty."

DeGrump's eyes darted the room, searching for an escape, for Razor, for anyone to come to fix the situation for him. But his only exit was blocked by my hulking figure radiating Yuletide fury. Razor sat petrified, clutching the booth like a drowning man clinging to a life raft.

"And then," I continued, my voice booming off the sweat-slick walls, "there's the little matter of your… 'holiday cheer' operation." My fist, usually filled with candy canes, crackled with frosty energy. "Seems like many of your employees are also on the naughty list and will receive a particularly nasty lump of coal this year, courtesy of you."

The insidious presence of meth had corrupted the festive cheer. Macon deGrump and his vile underboss, Razor, had turned this joyful season into a celebration of their toxic trade.

Macon deGrump's makeshift lab, hidden in the basement, was a factory that churned out meth, corroding bodies and minds and polluting the land with toxic chemicals. These assholes had turned my beloved Season into a vehicle of malevolent and poisonous profit.

What pissed me off the most was the erosion of the soul that meth wrought. My naughty list had been a lighthearted tradition, but now it served as a grim reminder of the souls ensnared by deGrump's web. These Santa-clad dealers, many of them also addicted, had abandoned their values and morals. They lied, stole, and addicted friends and family to feed their own habit, damaging themselves and bringing pain to those around them.

My anger burned with the intensity of a thousand Yule logs, fueled by the knowledge that the innocent were being led astray. The destructive nature of addiction that deGrump used for power and profit justified my rage, and I vowed to reclaim Christmas.

I lunged with a roar that shattered the glass windows and mirrors in the club. Catching my movement, Razor tried to rise, but a tendril of icy magic snaked out and slammed him back into the booth. DeGrump, cornered like a rat, tried to skitter away, but my fist, imbued with the fury of a thousand arctic blizzards, connected with his jaw.

Gone was jolly Santa. A whirlwind of Christmas fury stood in his place, a bringer of bitter justice. This year, the naughty list wouldn't just get coal. They'd get a taste of the North Pole's wrath. And for Razor and Macon deGrump, whom I observed regaining consciousness and slithering away to the back-office area of the club, I prayed this version of Christmas cheer might halt their evil actions and serve as a reminder to others of the consequences of bad choices.

I ripped my sack open, a feral roar erupting from my throat. Explosive gingerbread cookies, pulsating with frosty magic, rained down like miniature grenades. DeGrump's goons, those hulking slabs of misogyny, didn't stand a chance. The cookies detonated, showering them in a hail of shrapnel. The air crackled with a sickening sweetness— burnt gingerbread and fear.

Thick slabs of rock-hard gingerbread rained in a torrent through the club, punctuated by the crunch of splintered bone. The howls of my wounded enemies filled the air. My boots splashed through a puddle of blood with the viscosity of eggnog, leaving crimson footprints in my wake.

I whipped out my magic jump rope, the festive red and green turning into a blur of deadly intent as it whistled through the air, a serpent of Yuletide wrath. An obnoxious deGrump employee, his face twisted in a mask of drugged rage, caught its full brunt. The rope coiled around his legs, yanking him off his feet with a snap. He crumpled to the floor like a rag doll.

I waded deeper into the fray, and the magical toys of the

North Pole, once icons of hope and innocence, became instruments of righteous violence. Reaching into my bag, I removed a bundle of snow-riken—flat, razor-sharp, snowflake-shaped throwing stars—unleashing them into the necks, foreheads, and crotches of a dozen more inebriated purveyors of evil. This wasn't Santa Claus. This was vengeance incarnate. Let their screams be a chilling carol, I thought, a warning to those who dared defy the spirit of Christmas.

The air, reeking of blood and regurgitated alcohol, clawed at my throat when I passed. My boots crunched on glass and splintered wood, a grim counterpoint, along with my jingle bells, to the groans of the fallen. A tableau of my slaughter sprawled before me – a nightclub transformed into a battlefield. Instead of a thumping beat from the sound system, my heart, once a forge of Christmas cheer, hammered a dirge in my chest, and doubt coiled around my spirit like a python. Once a vibrant force, the light of the magic inside me began to sputter as my conviction faltered. This wasn't the bringer of merriment. This was a stranger whose eyes reflected the carnage surrounding him. Had I become the monster I sought to vanquish?

Memories of children's faces alight with hope flickered through my mind. The disappointment in their eyes would be a crueler fate than any blow. The jolly Santa, the guardian of innocence, was now a herald of violence.

Bloodstained and broken, I stood amidst the carnage I had wrought. The weight of my actions pressed down on me. Had I crossed a line from which there was no return?

Looking at the unconscious forms, I couldn't deny their wickedness. They were long-time residents on the naughty list, but did their darkness amplify the darkness that festered inside me?

The only thing colder than the steel in my heart was this terrifying realization: I may not be Santa Claus anymore.

Amid this mess, I saw Cinnamon, who had returned from evacuating the other dancers, her eyes reflecting my turmoil. We were two kindred spirits entangled in a web of vengeance. I could see the consequence of my actions, which resulted from her request, bearing down on her just as they were on me.

* * *

A mechanical groan, like a monstrous gearshift, broke the silence. Razor and deGrump and his goons weren't done. With a whirring hiss that sent shivers down my spine, two automated sentry guns appeared from behind the drapes on opposite sides of the wrecked nightclub – automated weapon systems mounted on sturdy poles, bristling with deadly intent. Red laser sights, malevolent eyes in the gloom, danced across the wreckage, seeking us out. Each sight pulsed with a vicious rhythm as high-caliber rounds chambered inside the guns – monstrously large bullets designed to obliterate anything they hit. I was cornered by a pair of robotic demons whose machinery thrummed with the promise of annihilation.

The world seemed to darken as I turned to Cinnamon, searching for answers in her eyes. Our alliance, born of rage and injustice, teetered on the brink of futility. I sank to my knees, my shoulders slumped in defeat. This was the end of my legacy, of everything I stood for, as deGrump returned and loomed above me. His smug smile widened as he saw the despair in my eyes; I felt my powers slipping away.

"Pathetic, old man," deGrump spat, his breath hot on my face, with Razor standing behind. "Who's the jolly one now?" His meaty hand drew back, ready to deliver a smashing blow. The twin red dots of laser sights danced across us. At least those turret guns won't fire on us, I thought, as long as he remains nearby.

Then, like an angel of chaos, Cinnamon burst into action. Her graceful, lithe form cut through the air as she launched herself from her new pole. Her caramel skin glistened with a sheen of perspiration. Her braids whipped around her as she wheeled with fluid precision. In that instant, I recognized her as an impressive woman and a force of nature.

I watched as she reached for a katana displayed behind the bar. God knows why there was a sword there – maybe deGrump fancied himself a wannabe samurai or member of the Yakuza—though he certainly wasn't. One-handed, in a sweeping arc, she quickly decapitated a Santa-suit-clad soldier, his head rolling down the bar like a bowling ball, his neck a fountain of red as his body stood headless for a few seconds before dropping to the floor.

Then I saw her fling the blade at another minion drawing a gun twenty feet away. The blade impaled him, pinning him to the wall like a thumbtack, where a stain of red darker than his Santa suit began spreading in a circle from his chest. As gravity pulled his body down the wall, the blade sliced his chest, neck, and head neatly in two until the two halves slowly pulled apart like a cast-off banana peel.

"Now's our chance, Santa!" Her strong voice was filled with a determination that seemed to come from deep within. She believed in me, even when I did not believe in myself. "Get up. We can still stop him!"

As Razor turned toward her, I saw the way his eyes lingered. He saw what I saw – a bold, fearless woman who radiated a fierce independence. She was not the timorous stripper he thought her to be.

Cinnamon undid the buttons of her blouse, revealing a toned midriff and firm, pear-shaped breasts, dark nipples like Hershey's kisses. When the fabric fell open, Razor's eyes went wide, fixating on her chest. Using his distraction, Cinnamon twirled, entangling the shirt around his legs. With a dancer's grace, each action deliberate and calculated, her lithesome body guided Razor's stumbling steps to the exact place where she could pivot and use his own strength against him, driving his skull through a bar table. His limp body lay unconscious on the floor, blood seeping from his ears.

"You won't keep me down!" I heard her shout, the words echoing through the club. With lightning-fast reflexes, I watched her dodge another thug's grasp, smashing a vodka bottle on the side of his head. "Your days of hurting people are over, deGrump!"

DeGrump sputtered, his face twisting with fury. He stepped toward Cinnamon, his eyes burning with rage. "You insolent little—"

"I'm not little!" she interrupted, her voice ringing clear. "I won't be silenced or exploited anymore. Santa and I stand for something bigger than your criminal empire. We stand for justice!"

Her words sparked something within me. As Cinnamon faced off against deGrump, I felt a glimmer of hope. Perhaps it wasn't too late. With Cinnamon by my side, we could turn the tide.

DeGrump's hand curled into a fist, and I knew he was about to strike. I wanted to move to protect Cinnamon, but my body felt heavy, and my magic seemed beyond reach. Had I indeed killed the magic of Christmas? My suit was now tattered and stained with the remnants of my rampage, the only sounds the labored breathing of injured fighters and the distant wail of sirens.

"The power of Christmas is still within you, Santa," Cinnamon's soft voice broke through, her calloused hand on my shoulder. "We can end this together." Her words were a balm, a draft of hot cocoa on a frosty night. I reached deep within myself, gathering every spark of magic I could muster, drawing upon the Season's power.

With an outstretched hand, I summoned the essence of arctic blizzards and howling winds until an icy blast surged forth, engulfing the turret guns in a dazzling display of frost and snow. The automated weapons crackled and froze, ice crystals spreading across their metal surfaces until they became immobilized, harmless sentries encased in a glittering cocoon. The air shimmered with the sound of cracking ice, punctuating the moment I stood tall, my magic reclaimed.

Together, we turned to face deGrump and his remaining minions. The room sizzled with tension, the flickering neon lights reflecting off their drawn guns and deGrump's gold chains.

DeGrump's eyes narrowed, his flushed face shifting from smugness to surprise. The once-powerful kingpin now stood diminished, his expensive suit ruined and bloodied. I felt a tiny rush of satisfaction, knowing we had disrupted his exploitative empire. But it wasn't enough.

Letting out a thunderous laugh that shook the foundations, I brandished a giant candy cane I'd plucked from my pocket, wielding it like a swordsman. In a blur of red and white stripes, I lunged at deGrump, my reflexes honed from years of high-speed toy deliveries, while he stumbled backward, his face contorting in fear.

Cinnamon moved in sync with me, her grace and agility fully displayed. She weaved through the thugs, delivering powerful kicks and elbow strikes with precision, each blow fueled by years of stifled anger and frustration. We were a whirlwind of color and motion—me, a burst of red, and she, a flashing comet of defiance.

I swung from a nearby pole, defying gravity as I launched myself into the heart of our enemies, skewering them with my razor-sharp candy cane weapon. Their screams were music to my ears. Cinnamon, a force of untamed fury, unleashed a high kick that would have made my elves proud. Her foot connected with deGrump's double chin, driving his head backward on his neck.

I delivered the coup de gras with a final flourish, impaling the long end of my candy cane through his ear, deep into his brain, swirling it around inside his grey matter for good measure. Looking up at me, I watched as the light faded from his eyes and his body slumped to the ground, joining his goons piled all around.

Cinnamon approached, her languid movement hinting at something. "Santa," she said softly, "I hope our paths cross again. Perhaps..." Her voice trailed off, leaving the sentence unfinished as her index finger slowly traced the lapel of my red suit south toward my thick black belt.

Having borne the journey of the night's events, my heart now swelled with an ardor that extended from my red, rosy nose to my toes, hitting all the right places in between. The magic within me pulsed, reminding me of my responsibilities—the gifts to deliver, the joy to spread, and the world to remind me of the true spirit of Christmas. But at that moment, all I could see was Cinnamon.

We embraced, and her petite frame fit perfectly against me. "Cinnamon," I said. "Would you consider joining me on my deliveries? We could make it a date."

Cinnamon squeezed me tighter inside her sinewy arms. "A date it is, Santa," she answered, her eyes sparkling. "I know we have a tight deadline tonight, but can I ask that we visit my place when we are finished? There is someone special I'd like you to meet—my daughter Ava. I want to give her the gift of believing in Christmas again."

How could I refuse? The prospect of bringing cheer to

Cinnamon and her child filled me with lightness and hope. And so, we stepped out into the winter night, the stars winking in approval.

"A special visit it shall be," I assured her, my eyes twinkling in delight. We'll bring Christmas cheer to the rest of the world first, then celebrate together, just you, me, and Ava."

So, Santa and Cinnamon, an unlikely duo, embarked on a magical journey, spreading joy to the farthest reaches of the globe and then to each other. And that is how we became partners in hope, love, and the true spirit of Christmas.

A Christmas Wish
M.J. McClymont

The ground trembled as an articulated vehicle rumbled past, its tyres sluicing filth and slush to the side of the road. Officer Harrison Wish raised a hand in greeting, a gesture the driver returned.

Wish pulled the scarf tighter round his neck and stamped his feet in a bid to keep the blood circulating. A short distance to his left stood Joe Morris, gripping the portable LiDAR gun in one trembling hand. Wish could see the drifting plumes of his partner's exhalations emerging through the woollen material of his scarf, which he had tugged up over his nose and mouth, and he wondered how much longer it would be before Morris would toss him the LiDAR and retreat into the car again. He didn't blame him; the nip in the air was becoming painful now despite the layers he wore.

"You surviving there, Morris?" Wish continued to stamp his feet like a gull attracting worms.

"Barely. I could snap a finger off for each thing I'd rather be doing on Christmas Eve. Reckon someone in the office has got it in for us?"

The glaring headlights of a black BMW flicked from full beam to dipped, indicating that the driver had spied the officers and identified their reflective garb. Wish smiled wanly. He didn't want to hand out tickets tonight. Something about delaying workers on their way home from the office to spend the festive period with loved ones somehow felt wrong.

"Nah," he said at last. "We just pulled the short straw, that's all. It'll be some other poor bugger's turn next year."

Morris snorted. "Yeah, right, we'll see. I'm sure you'd rather be at home with the missus, eh?"

The thought of languishing in the heat with someone who actually felt some affection for him drew a pang of longing. He had been posted at the back of beyond, on a road rarely used, hemmed in on both sides by rows of naked birch and elm. Now that autumn's splendour was spent, the tall trunks had split into bare black branches reaching into the starry sky like skeletal hands clutching at diamonds. A cloak of darkness had fallen at around five in the afternoon, aiding the drop in temperature. Wish knew that the temperature at home in Anna's company would be just as icy.

"We're, erm, well we're not exactly seeing eye to eye."

"Trouble in paradise, eh?"

Wish shook his head, cursing himself for letting his mouth run. These weren't things you discussed with workmates. His father, a stern and stoic man, had raised him to remain stolid against life's slings and arrows; to deal with emotions internally, inside the bone trap of his mind where they belonged, not to spill his feelings over the first pair of willing ears.

"Something like that," said Wish, hoping that Morris would sense his reticence to elucidate and drop the subject, thereby ridding Wish of the increasing compulsion to unburden himself. His hopes were dashed a moment later.

"I thought you two were solid as a rock."

Wish opened his mouth and then closed it. He stamped his feet a few times and crossed his arms, digging his gloved hands into his armpits in an attempt to generate a smidgen more heat. A part of his mind, the part that retained the essence of his father's nature warned him to keep his trap shut, but his heart ached and the temptation to shrug the weight off his shoulders proved too much to suppress. "She's having an affair, Joe."

Morris's arm dropped as though the weight of the LiDAR had become too much for him. He faced Wish. A beat up Kia shot past them slicing the air with a strident susurration and throwing up a shower of ice and mud. Morris seemed not to notice. "No," he said. "Are you sure…?"

"I'm certain," Wish interjected. "I've read the messages on her phone. The guy sent her photos of his… you know." The memory of his own actions caused him a passing twinge of shame. He knew that trawling through Anna's messages had been a terrible breach of trust but he felt he already knew, he just needed to see the evidence to be certain.

Morris ran a hand down his face and shook his head as though dispelling an unpleasant mental image. "That's, um, yep, that's pretty damning. Do you," Morris cleared his throat. "Do you know who he is?"

"There's no name attached to the number."

Morris pulled his scarf down, blew a plume of warm breath into the air and scratched the dark stubble underlining his angular jaw. "Could it have been a wrong number?"

Wish shook his head.

"I'm sorry, pal. If you ever find out, and you want to go to the guy's door, take him for a spin, put the shitters up him, I'm with you."

"Thanks, Morris, but it's not revenge I'm after. I just want things back the way they were. I'd forgive and forget, if I thought that's what she wanted, but it doesn't appear to be and anyway, I don't even know how to broach the subject."

"Well, if you're sure."

"I'm sure."

Morris shrugged. "You always were a boring bastard, Wish."

Wish smirked at this, eliciting a peel of laughter from Morris. After a brief pause, Wish joined in. To laugh was to defy darkness, both inside and out. The darkness inside him waned a little in contrast to the darkness around him, which only deepened.

After a brief thaw in the car with the heating turned up and a mug of sweet, black coffee from the thermos Morris had prepared, Wish felt ready to resume his duties. He lifted the LiDAR and took his position by the side of the road, waiting for passing traffic while Morris remained in the car sipping his second mug of coffee.

He heard it before he could see it; the sound of bells, sleigh bells jangling accompanied by a scraping, grinding cacophony. Morris had left the headlights of their vehicle on, but it was facing the opposite direction so he couldn't yet see the source of the din. Wish waved his arms at his partner but Morris wasn't paying attention, his eyes were fixed upon the glowing screen of his phone. Wish turned on the light on the chest of his fleece and produced a compact metal torch from his pocket.

In the distance, a single, lambent light flickered as it swung from side to side. The darkened silhouette of a vehicle being led by a group of quadrupeds, their antlers waving, drew near. Wish glanced back at the car, to Morris and this time he managed to catch his eye. Morris opened the driver's door of the car.

"Give the siren a blast, Morris."

"Eh, why?"

"Just bloody do it."

The strident whoop of the siren seemed to have the desired effect. The vehicle slowed and came to a grinding halt next to Wish. The carriage had no wheels, just twin blades running the length of the chasse which had no doubt scored the road. The driver, swathed in shadow, released the reigns tethered to the reindeer and fixed his attentions on Wish. "Is there a problem, officer?" he crooned in a silky, condescending tone.

"Several," said Wish, "starting with you tearing up the blacktop in this contraption, which, might I add, is clearly not roadworthy. Mind stepping out where I can see you?"

The figure emerged from the sleigh. He was tall, abnormally tall, Wish reckoned around seven feet tall, and he wore a Santa Claus outfit. The hat, a long coat that reached his knees, boots and trousers held up by braces which looped over his bare shoulders. Wish could see the man's ribs jutting against the mottled flesh of his chest like rubber pulled taut over narrow slats. Beneath the stained rim of his hat, the man regarded him from deep dark sockets, in a narrow, heavily lined face. The dimensions of his face were all wrong and Wish wondered if some sort of deformity was responsible for his unsettling appearance.

"Been celebrating have we, sir?"

"If you mean, have I been consuming alcohol, then no, officer, I have not. Alcohol is not my poison of choice."

Wish raised an eyebrow, feigning interest. "Really? What is your poison?"

"The suffering and agony of those whose transgressions cause misery to others, particularly at this most joyous time of the year. And perhaps a little crystal meth."

"Right you are, sir." Wish raised an eyebrow. He wanted to laugh at the ridiculousness of it, but a trickle of fear prevented him from doing so.

The tall man shrugged his robe up his shoulders. Gnarled, elongated hands ending in knife-like fingernails protruded from the filthy white sleeves of the robe. Beneath the Santa Claus hat, yellow eyes glared with intensity, set deep into a frightful countenance. The giant's ruined nose, no more than two uneven slits flared as he grinned down at

Wish, narrow, brown stained shards protruded at obtuse angles from blackened gums like sewing needles stuck, eye down, into a charred pincushion.

Wish cleared his throat. "What's with the outfit?"

"This is no outfit, officer, it is a uniform." The giant's eyes twitched as he scanned Wish like a predator weighing up its prey. Wish turned his head, seeking verification that his partner would have his back if things happened to go pear shaped; something he was beginning to believe could be a very real eventuality. Morris stood behind him in silent awe.

"That's enough nonsense, I want direct answers, understand?"

The giant nodded. "Of course."

"What's your name?"

"Santa Claus."

"Last warning."

"Miles Gann."

"Address, Mister Gann?"

"My address, officer?"

Wish dropped a hand over his taser and glared at Gann.

"Here and there. Of no fixed abode, shall we say? Laterally, I have been living in an old flat above a closed record shop in the city…"

"Edinburgh?"

"No, London. But I vacated the premises three weeks ago to prepare for the festive season. It's my busiest time of the year, you know." Gann pinched the furred edge of his coat between a slender thumb and forefinger and gave it a tug.

"Dare I ask your occupation, Mister Gann?"

"Oh, this and that."

The officer sighed wearily. "You're Miles Gann, you live here and there and you do this and that, that's what we're going with, is it?"

"That is correct, officer."

Wish shook his head and looked at Morris, who didn't appear to be listening. His partner had left his side and was standing in front of the sleigh, his head turning left and right like a spectator at a tennis match as he examined the tethered beasts. Wish wanted to believe that they were reindeer, but he had never laid eyes on deer that big or with jet black pelt before. Their milky white eyes fixed forward as though completely unaware of Morris's presence. "Are these reindeer?" Asked Morris.

"Of a sort," said the giant. "They are from, shall we say, down south."

When one of the beasts snorted, Morris flinched and the tall man let out a deep, rumbling chuckle. As unnerving as the encounter was, Wish felt a burning streak of anger towards Gann. The tall man was clearly making fun of them.

While Wish tamped down his fizzling rage, a warbling moan emanated from the rear of the sleigh, behind the front bench. Wish craned his neck over the side and stumbled back when a large sack lurched towards him. He approached again with care. "Is there someone in there?" He knew the question was stupid but he had no intentions of taking risks. He reached out tentatively.

"I wouldn't do that if I were you, officer," said Gann.

"What's in the sack, Gann?"

"An undesirable, a very naughty individual. You know the type, I'm sure you deal with them all the time."

The sack tumbled and a series of frantic moans followed.

"Morris, cuff this idiot."

Morris stepped forward, eyeing Gann, ready to respond accordingly to any display of resistance, but Gann merely turned and allowed the officer to restrain him. All the while he grinned like a lunatic and glared at Wish from beneath the furry brim of his ridiculous red hat.

Wish loosened the rope tied around the neck of the sack and darted back when it birthed the bald head and shoulders of a naked, gagged and bound middle-aged man. The man stared at Wish, the furrows on his forehead deep, his eyes beseeching, mist ejected from his flared nostrils hung in the air between them before drifting off. Behind Wish, Gann emitted another obnoxious giggle. A sound, which to Wish, appeared strange and otherworldly.

"Right, let's get you in the car. It seems there are a few questions that need answered," said Morris. Gann nodded obediently and began to walk ahead of Morris towards the glaring headlights of the car.

The naked man shook uncontrollably, his sights never leaving the tall red phantasm that seemed to glide past. He flinched and let out a squeal of fright when Gann shot him a fleeting glance.

"It's alright," said Wish. "You're safe now." He stepped into the sleigh and helped the man out of the sack. The man's paunch wobbled when he stumbled free. Wish attempted to untie the bonds his arms had been trussed with but they had been pulled taught needed to be severed. The bindings around the bottom half of his face had similarly been pulled tight. Wish draped the sack over the man's shoulders. "Stay here," he said. "I'm going to get you some blankets and hot coffee. We'll get you warmed up and back home in no time."

The man nodded, still staring at Gann. When Wish turned to fetch blankets from the trunk of the car he heard a scraping sound coming from the direction of the sleigh. This was followed by the rapid patter of footsteps. Wish spun in time to see the naked man running, hands still bound behind his back, towards the woods, his bare buttocks trembled like separate fleshy jellies as he pelted into the tree line and was swallowed by darkness.

"Shit," spat Wish. At the car, Morris was folding Gann's towering frame into the back seat. "You go this, Morris?"

"Yep, get after him."

Wish didn't have to be told twice, he plunged into the inky gloom after Gann's naked victim. The beam of his standard issue torch penetrated the shadows and it didn't take long to locate the man. He found him cowering behind the thick trunk of a beech tree.

"Calm down, you're going to be okay," Wish said, holding a hand out in order to assuage his fear.

"Can you really guarantee that, Officer Wish?"

Wish's heart lurched in his chest and he turned quickly, almost losing his balance. Gann stood a few feet away peering down at him. One bracelet of the cuffs Morris had restrained him with still encircled on wrist. The attached metal had been twisted and snapped. A high pitched moan of terror came from the naked man behind Morris. Gann stepped past Wish, the officer flinched as he came close. Gann gripped the rear of the man' neck and steered him into the torch light.

"How… how did you… where's Officer Morris?"

Gann shrugged and waved a clawed hand in the air.

Wish removed his Taser and prepared the weapon. "What do you want with this man?"

"I want nothing. Like I say, he's been a very naughty boy this year, Officer Wish." Gann said, resting a gnarled, oversized hand on his victim's shoulder. The man jumped and moaned through the strip of cloth covering his mouth. "You've seen some things during your tenure, I imagine, and I guarantee you've heard worse than you've seen. Now imagine the most repulsive act your desensitised mind can possibly muster." The spectre raised a single talon and scratched its head with it before letting it drop heavily by its side.

Wish aimed the Taser. "I'm warning you, Mister Gann. Let him go or I will taser you."

Gann threw its head back and let out a distorted bellow of mirth. Wish fired the Taser. The giant did not appear to notice the fifty thousand volts coursing through its body. Far from incapacitated, he dropped a curled hand and bought it up with lightening speed, eviscerating the naked man trembling next to him.

The man let out a muffled scream, his eyes wide, staring

down in abject terror at his innards unfurled from the wound in his abdomen. He dropped to his knees, landing in the ropy mass of intestine, his screeching pleas for mercy echoed through the woods.

Stumbling back, Wish let out a loud, grating roar of fright which began in the pit of his belly, propelled by the contracting of his diaphragm. His breathing came in rushed, labouring wheezes and his heart stuttered beneath his ribcage. "Why, why, why?"

Gann appeared to find Wish's horrified mantra amusing. He grinned and plucked the barbed tips of the taser bolt from his withered chest and then he stooped down to face the officer. The stink of his breath washed over him; a miasma of rotting meat and sulphur. Wish gagged and held up an ineffectual, defensive hand, palm out.

"It would be a lie to say I do not take any pleasure in this, officer, but if you must know, I am merely doing my duty, delivering a gift."

"A gift?" Wish covered his mouth with his hand. With the other, he pushed the button on his radio. Another burst of static sounded and nothing more.

"Yes, Officer Wish. I deliver gifts to those who have suffered at the hands of others. I assumed my role was clear to you."

Wide eyed and terrified, Wish shook his head.

"Is there something you would ask of me? Something to ease your pain?"

Wish shook his head again and then stopped. He thought some more. "N-no."

"Something, I think. I can smell your suffering; its fragrance is familiar to me." Gann said, producing a tattered notepad and feather fountain pen from the folds of his robe. "I can end it for you. All you have to do it write it here. Needless to say, there will be no repercussions for you and you will never see me again."

Wish considered this. Yes, he had suffered, he was still suffering. Every moment he spent in his home with the woman he had chosen to live out his years with, the woman who now shunned him, seemed like torture. Knowing that Anna's affections presently made someone else feel the way he once felt created a void in his heart. Not only had be lost his wife, he had lost a major part of his himself, now all that remained were the fragments of a former existence, before Anna, that he would have to mould into some semblance of a life.

Wish took the pen with a trembling hand. The tip scraped the page as he wrote and when he had finished, the scrawled words faded, leaving the page blank once again. Wish stood for the longest time, listening to crunch of bracken beneath Gann's boots as he retreated.

Silence reigned in the shadows where moonlight surrendered to gloom. Cracks in the canopy above projected a shattered pale glow upon the torn corpse of the naked man; the man who, in life, had allegedly performed an unknown repulsive act. Wish no longer cared to understand the fine points of this transgression. He wanted to be at home where he would be shunned but safe and warm.

He lingered on the edge of the tree line for a time until he was certain the Gann had left. When he saw that the sleigh was gone and there was no sign of the giant, he headed for the car. Upon his approach, he realised that Morris was gone too. The rear passenger door of the car lay upon the frosted ground, twisted and broken.

Raising his hands to either side of his mouth, he shouted out. "MORRIS!" His call was absorbed by the night and no reply was forthcoming.

"JOE!"

Silence.

He slipped his phone out of his pocket and rang Morris's number. The recorded message told him that the person he was calling could not be contacted. After a final cursory scan of his immediate surroundings, Wish called the office and requested to be patched through to the duty sergeant. He provided the basics, his mind sluggish with too many thoughts being processed at once. The voice at the other end of the line demanded more information, launching a rapid fire assault of questions like gunshots. It was only to be expected; he had just reported the body of a slaughtered John Doe, and a missing officer- nothing like this had ever happened before- nothing like this should ever happen.

He slumped against the car and slid down until his rump rested upon the chilled ground. The gap between his ear and the phone widened. He strained to identify intelligible words in the sub-audible rumble coming from the handset and then he stopped listening altogether.

It wasn't long before the distant warble of approaching

sirens echoed in the night.

* * *

Wish woke around ten AM, prompted by horrific mental snapshots of the previous night's shift. He had finally arrived back at the office at around two AM and remained there, carefully tying a redacted version of his report. Feeling a great deal of concern for Morris, he offered to join the search for his partner, an offer that was rejected when the duty sergeant ordered him to return home. He had pleaded his case, pointing out that Joe was not just a colleague, but a friend. His objection was overruled and he was chased from the office.

A stray stab of guilt assaulted his conscience when he entertained that possibility that Anna's lover may have been, or could be at that very moment, intimidated by the giant terror Santa. Perhaps Gann was uttering detailed threats of bodily harm in his silky tones to a stalk eyed, dick pic dealing piece of shit. He dismissed this rumination. To hell with him, he had made his bed, in Wish's marital bed; whatever happened how was of no consequence to Wish.

He glanced over at the opposite side of the bed, the empty side and sighed deeply. "Merry Christmas," he muttered, dropping his legs over the side of the mattress and making his way downstairs for coffee.

He entered the sitting room tentatively, nodding to Anna and uttered a festive greeting which was not reciprocated. He knew that their relationship was truly over. Strings tethered to the ball of lead which had settled in his stomach, tugged on his heart, reminding him what true sadness felt like. It would only be a matter of time now before she finally admitted to him how she felt and broke the news of the new flame in her life. Wish surmised that she would wait until the festive period was over before coming clean.

On the wall above the bookcase, a monochrome canvas photograph from their wedding day hung; just the two of them, holding hands and gazing into each other's eyes. With a spreading feeling of loss came the realisation that she would never look at him in that way again. That smile belonged to someone else now.

"Good morning. Merry Christmas," he repeated.

Anna's sight remained fixed on the television in the corner. "Coffee in the pot."

"Thanks."

"I thought we agreed, Harrison," said Anna, not deigning to look at her husband.

"Agreed?"

"Yes, we agreed, no gifts."

"We did," Wish confirmed, puzzled.

She sighed. "Then what's this?"

On the coffee table before her sat a neatly wrapped parcel, complete with bow. Wish glanced at it with little interest. "A Christmas present?" he said.

"We agreed, no gifts," Anna repeated.

"It's not from me, love. I got home at just before three this morning. I've been working all night. Perhaps it's from… what's his name?"

Anna threw him a sharp look, averting her eyes just as

quickly. The look of guilt was as clear as the glass top of the table on which the mystery parcel sat. Wish had seen that look a thousand times. A strange urge to laugh overcame him. The incongruity of such a compulsion eased the burden of loss somewhat. He resisted it deftly with an expression hewn from stone.

"Would you like me to fetch scissors?" Wish asked.

"I can unwrap a bloody present, Harrison."

He pressed his lips together and nodded. He had been through enough failed relationships to realise that Anna's hostility was purposeful, forced. Whenever a relationship crumbles, both parties exaggerate their dislike of one another. In some cases, it acts as a defence mechanism, in most cases, no matter how amicable the split is, it was the only way for a former couple to move past their vacillations and eradicate any vestige of lingering mutual fondness, thereby providing finality to their dissolution. It was a sad state of affairs, but Wish had decided some time ago that he would not be a party to petty squabbles and snarky verbal jabs.

In the kitchen, Wish poured a mug of steaming black coffee and returned to the sitting room. Anna had torn the paper off the parcel and was prying the flaps of the cardboard box apart. Wish watched with interest as she popped the black plastic bag inside the box and tore it open.

When she screamed, Wish dropped his mug. The contents leapt out, scalding his foot and he hissed in pain. Anna scrambled across the couch, burying her back against the cushioned armrest and began to moan, her eyelids peeled back from her protuberant eyes which remained fixed on the box.

Wish followed her stare. He could see a tuft of black hair protruding from the torn mass of opaque plastic like burnt grass surrounding a campfire, but he didn't have to look any further to figure out what the box contained.

Is there something you would ask of me?

Wish shuddered at the memory and approached the box.

Although he hadn't asked for death, he now realised that the naked man's demise should have given some indication of how his Christmas request would be executed.

Something to ease your suffering?

He could see the pale nub of a nose protruding from the waxen face of the severed head. The head of his wife's lover, the man whose filthy messages he had secretly perused on his wife's phone. The gift hadn't been for Anna after all, it was Wish's special Christmas gift.

Wish edged his way between the coffee table and the couch, stopping directly in front of the box and with mounting reticence, he tore the plastic that away from the bottom half of the victim's face. He stared down at the gruesome contents of the box, and deep into the pale blue, lifeless eyes of Joe Morris.

Hadley's Hope
E. Catherine Tobler

"You can't just say it like that."

"Yes, yes I can."

Frederick Hadley listened to his parents arguing, but he had missed the subject entirely, so he wasn't quite sure what his mother was objecting to. He pressed his ear harder against the kitchen door, but there was a lull in the argument. He could hear only his mother's acrylic nails tap tap tapping on the counter.

"It's settled then," his father said.

"Yes," his mother said.

Footsteps then, coming toward the door. Frederick scampered down the hall and back to the living room, where his sister Taylor was stringing popcorn. More of the popcorn was winding up in her mouth than on the string, and they certainly didn't have a Christmas tree to hang the popcorn strings on. Stringing the corn, their father had said, was its own joy. Was it, though?

"It's time we all stopped pretending," their father said as he strode into the room. He commanded every inch of the space, so much so that Frederick sucked in a breath. His father had taken all the air away. "Despite what you see outside every day, it is vital that you understand. Santa Claus does not exist."

Frederick's eyes flit from father to mother—mother who stood unmoving like she had been carved from ice. Frederick could not read her expression, but remembered the kitchen argument. She'd told father not to say it like that. Frederick looked at Taylor, who was gnawing on a string of popcorn. She was only six—what did she know about anything? Frederick was nine, and that was ages older.

"He *does*," Frederick said. "You told us so—that he brings the gifts and that our cookie and milk offerings are an equit—" Oh, he struggled with that word.

"Equitable exchange," his father said. He sank onto the couch beside little Taylor, and pulled the string of corn from between her lips. "Sometimes we eat your cardboard cookies, but we pour the milk back into the carton."

Frederick's eyes flicked back to his mother, but she had not moved. Whatever argument she had provided against this in the kitchen showed no sign of appearing in the living room. George looked at his wife, as if to ascertain this was so. Frederick recognized only the chill in his father's eyes.

"We buy and wrap the gifts and tell you they came from a stranger," his father continued. "You believe a fat white man travels the entire world in the course of a single night— with flying reindeer."

"Well." Frederick had believed it—with his whole heart. It was the one thing he was certain of. "*You* told us—"

"Myth and legend," his mother finally said. She did not,

however, move from her position in the doorway. "Like any other story we've told you. Boy wizards aren't real. Talking cats aren't real." She crossed her arms over her chest and pinned Frederick with a look he did not recognize from her. She had always been the warm one before now. "Boys never run away to the carnival and live forever."

It was as if she had upended his entire bookshelf and set the books on fire and danced in the ashes. Frederick took a breath, because he didn't feel like he had been breathing at all. The room was getting dark at the edges, the air beginning to hiss.

Taylor began to softly cry.

* * *

Come morning, outside was glazed in ice and snow. Frederick's boot slipped when he climbed into the SUV; he wasn't feeling too sharp, having been kept awake by noises on the roof that couldn't possibly have been reindeer, given it wasn't Christmas Eve, nor did Santa exist.

Taylor was already belted into the backseat. His school was closer though, so his father would drop him first. Frederick stole a glance at his father, who did not look away from the road. Frederick wanted to ask questions—about Christmas, about Santa Claus—but he kept quiet, watching the neighborhood instead.

Their house stood undecorated, while all those around them were trimmed in wreaths and come night, lights. Reindeer stood unlit on snowy lawns, but every picket fence and gate were trimmed with greenery, with holly and ivy, and silver bells. These things did not represent Santa Claus so much as they did Christmas, but Frederick felt a loss even so. Myths and legends, his mother had said, but last year—hadn't they left cookies and milk and—

Cardboard. Poured back in the carton.

Frederick held his backpack against his chest. Soon enough, they pulled into the school grounds, and the engine idled while Frederick did not move. When he looked at his father, there was a scowl.

"You're about to make your sister late," his father said, "is that what you want?"

It was better not to want things, Frederick thought. He glanced back at his sister, who gave him a bright smile. She was only six, but he knew that smile; it was secretive and spoke of mischief.

"No, sir," Frederick murmured, and he unhooked his seatbelt and slid from the car. The moment he had closed the door, his father pulled away.

Frederick stood where he had gotten out, in a cloud of exhaust. Students who were allowed to walk came up the sidewalks, and headed into the school, but Frederick stared after the SUV until he could no longer see it.

"Ain't coming back for you."

Jeremy was Frederick's age, but taller, and Frederick looked into his eyes, wanting to punch the smug smile off his face. "Do you believe in Santa?" he asked instead.

Confusion flicked through Jeremy's eyes, and the boy took a step backward. "Don't say that name," he said, then turned and hurried into the school.

In the school halls, Frederick paid closer attention to the

decorations. Every room was trimmed, in garland and greenery. Calendars had days marked with bells or wreaths. Cut-out paper decorations illustrated snowmen or penguins, and mobiles of snowflakes dangled from every ceiling. Frederick's class had cut snowflakes the day before, taping them to the classroom windows. But nowhere, he realized, was there an image of Santa Claus. There were no images of Rudolph, or elves, or anything else that might be connected to the North Pole. Snow was generic, Frederick decided, as likely in their town as it was at the North Pole. It wasn't Santa related, not really.

Frederick busied himself with science, and social studies, and reading, and then it was lunch, and he looked for Jeremy in the cafeteria. He wasn't alone, but sitting with Kelsey and David. Frederick joined them without an invitation, and they all looked at him as if he had interrupted something.

"Are you Jewish?" Kelsey asked without preamble.

"That can't be it," David said before Frederick could. "They had decorations up last year, didn't they?" His dark eyes pinned Frederick. "Didn't you?"

Frederick was certain they had, but after the last few hours, he was beginning to doubt his own memory. "Y-yes?"

"A question can't be an answer," David said.

Frederick shoved a spoonful of chili into his mouth and chewed, watching the others. Jeremy hadn't said a word. Frederick took a much-too-large bite of cinnamon roll and nodded a little bit.

"Yeah," he said around the mouthful, "this year, it was just too much. Grandma died and they didn't want to decorate, but me and Tay are stringing popcorn." Frederick nodded. His grandmother had not, in fact, died, but it sounded reasonable, that death would preclude decorations.

The trio sat with that a moment. David shoveled more chili into his mouth, Kelsey pulled a finger through the glaze on her roll, and Jeremy sucked his milk carton dry.

"Listen," Frederick said to Jeremy, "about Santa—"

Jeremy's hand came down hard on the table and Frederick felt the turn of every eye in the cafeteria toward them.

"I said not to say that name."

"Okay, but..." Frederick was about to say it again, but given the look in Jeremy's eyes, he swallowed it. Jeremy was shaking. "About the decorations." He'd try that way, maybe. "There aren't any of—"

Jeremy pushed away from the table, collected his tray, and left. David bolted after him, leaving his half-eaten lunch, but Kelsey stayed, sliding over to occupy the seat Jeremy had vacated.

"There aren't any of Santa," she whispered.

The hair on Frederick's arms stood up. "Right, that." He looked around the cafeteria, and while the monitors were watching Jeremy and David rush away, they weren't paying much attention to him and Kelsey. He hunkered back down beside her. "What's that about?"

"Just stories," Kelsey said. "You don't see Jesus

decorations at Easter, do you?"

Frederick turned that over in his head. "That's different." He didn't know how it was different, only that it was. He ate more chili and cinnamon roll, then pushed his tray away when Kelsey hadn't said anything else. "If Santa doesn't exist, why do they tell us he does?"

"Jesus," Kelsey said again.

But she whispered it this time, and her voice wavered, and Frederick didn't like the look in her eyes, the way she kind of disconnected from him or anything else and was in her own place. She was looking entirely at something else—something he couldn't see.

"Kel."

"Gotta go."

She got up from the table and didn't take her tray and so Frederick bussed the entire table, under the eye of the monitors all the while. He smiled at them when he left, and followed the long curving hallway to the library. He had a few minutes before class and just wanted to look.

Every book he looked in, though, made no mention of Santa, and by the time he was walking back to his classroom, he had begun to wonder if he was somehow sick. He didn't feel unreasonably hot or unreasonably cold, but he was shaking all over and felt strange in the pit of his stomach. He kept quiet in class, trying to pay attention, but he didn't care too much for math, when he was trying to figure out—

What was it? Not math but... For a minute, Frederick couldn't remember, then the name came rushing back. Santa Claus. He opened his notebook and carefully wrote it down, having some trouble adding the last name when he did. It was ridiculous, he decided by the time they were gathering their things to head home. Jeremy was playing a joke on him, taking something normal and twisting it—and probably so were his parents. Santa isn't real, they said and softly laughed, all the while knowing this Christmas would be the best Christmas ever and they would wake up to towers of wrapped boxes and bulging stockings.

In the afternoons, Frederick was allowed to walk home; it was two blocks south and one block east, and he had memorized the way long, long ago. But today, the streets looked different. He wasn't sure how. Sure, there was snow, but it was beginning to melt. And sure, there were decorations, and sure, none of them contained jolly, fat men, but so what? Frederick found, though, that when he looked at the street signs, he had gone three blocks south.

The streets were easy, named for trees, so he thought to backtrack—just one street back would put him on Pine, and Pine was where he was meant to be, but when he looked at the green and white street sign, it said Mapleton. He walked one more street and it said Spruce. Pine should have been between those.

Frederick stood, shaking. He wasn't old enough for a phone yet, his parents kept saying, so he had no way to call—and besides, dad would still be at work. Mom would be home, but dad had the car.

He walked back one more street, and it still didn't say Pine. It said Mapleton. The corner house was the same, with its little manger, and Frederick's heart leaped at the sight of it. Jesus decorations—he had to tell Kelsey. He walked up the lawn, shoes crunching the snow, and peered down into the manger, but where there should have been a baby Jesus, there was a carefully wrapped bundle. It was pale, oval and long like bread, but wrapped in something black, that looked like silk. But when the thing moved, it moved like oil, flowing and not solid. The bundle squirmed and the edge of whatever it had been wrapped in slid away, revealing—

"You there!"

Frederick's head came up sharply at the voice—a man, standing on the porch, holding a rifle. *Ah shit*, Frederick thought, and figured he would be grounded for the curse, even though it had only been a thought.

"Put baby Jesus back."

"I didn't—"

Frederick was about to say he hadn't taken the baby Jesus, when the oily thing in the manger touched him. Frederick shrieked and fled down the lawn, stumbling through the snow. Given the weight of his backpack, he went face-first into the snow; the coldness pressed into his nose, against his eyes, and he screamed again, because it felt like the oily thing against his hand. Cold and sharp and—

He rolled and kicked. Snow exploded around him and he thought the man had fired the rifle, but once he'd regained his feet, he could see it was only him in the snow, thrashing like he meant to make the most metal snow angel of all time. The man on the porch was staring, but Frederick didn't stop. He ran, ran to where Pine should have been, and it was there, and he clung to the pole that held the street sign. For a breath, the world stopped tipping out from under him.

"Frederick?"

He opened his eyes to see Mrs. Adams there, her car idling at the stop sign. Frederick couldn't manage a smile for her, even though she looked quite concerned.

"Do you need a ride home, dear?"

Frederick was about to shake his head, but when Mrs. Adams opened the passenger door, he got into the car, and belted himself in. She smelled like face powder and apples and Frederick closed his eyes.

"Let's get you home," she said. "It's almost time for Santa."

Frederick's skin prickled. Mrs. Adams drove and he looked at her, offering a trembling smile when she gave him one.

"W-what do you know about Santa?" he asked.

"Only the usual things," she said. "He sees you when you're sleeping—he knows when you're awake." She never took her eyes from the road, hands at two and ten. "You're what now, nine? That's about the right age. My boys were eight and nine, if I remember right."

"The right age?" Frederick pressed himself more deeply into the car seat, but his pants squished beneath him, sodden from the roll in the snow.

Mrs. Adams's smile was a sad one. "To learn the truth about Santa Claus."

When she didn't say any more, Frederick was too stunned to press her for information. His parents had said

Santa didn't exist, was a myth, but Kelsey understood that something else was going on—but what.

She let him out when they reached his house, and she gave him another sad smile "Once you know the truth…"

But she didn't finish, and pulled away, and Frederick stood there in his wet pants, wondering what the whole thing meant. Her boys, she'd said. But Frederick had never seen her with children—she was old enough to be his grandmother, so her kids were probably old too. Frederick was no closer to sorting it when he walked into the kitchen. His mother immediately began to holler—how *dare* he come into the house looking like he'd been rolling in the snow. Well, he had been, so.

That night, he wanted very much to ask his parents about Santa, but they kept looking at him as if they expected him to ask and were prepared to explode if he did. Instead, he asked for an hour of screen time, to research his end-of-semester report for school, and was only mildly annoyed that his parents agreed to thirty-five minutes. Frederick opened the laptop in the family room, his mother occupied in the kitchen (it was cookies tonight, and he was too excited for them), his father busy with a televised football game only a few chairs away. Taylor was playing Barbies, and Frederick had to open his notebook to remember the name he wanted to type into the search bar.

S-A-N-T-A C-L-A-U-S.

Frederick scrolled past the immediate advertisements for reindeer leggings and sexy ugly Christmas sweaters. The first link took him to Wikipedia, showing him the image of a jolly, fat white man. It could have been his grandfather, really. Frederick read, and read some more, and three paragraphs in, his mild annoyance at his limited screen time had deepened. The article confirmed that Santa was a myth, "a legendary character," it said. Like something you might meet in a video game. An end boss, Frederick thought, and peered around the screen to be sure his father was still occupied.

Wikipedia was useless, though; it didn't tell Frederick anything useful. Even the section that detailed criticisms about Santa was annoying. They all came back to Jesus, and he wondered if Kelsey was on to something there, after all. The Wikipedia entry on Jesus was even less helpful; by the time he finished, Frederick definitely thought it also should have been tagged "a legendary character."

Frederick came to the end of his screen time having learned little that was helpful. His mother took the laptop away and gave him a cookie in exchange, but the frosting was hard and the cookie crumbled, and nothing felt right. The streets had been out of order and baby Jesus had been a monster. All babies are monsters, Kelsey said when he asked her about it the next day, but she had a baby sister so had feelings about the whole thing. Still, her eyes told him something he couldn't understand.

"What—"

"Sssh."

Winter break came as it always did and Frederick managed to lose himself in the wonder of it all for a little while. Twenty-four inches of snow had him and Jeremy building snow forts between their lawns, losing action figures amid the white hills. Maybe they'd find them come spring, but for now, the loss was tragic, the other figures lined on the drifted plains to funeral them away.

But soon enough, Christmas Eve arrived, and Frederick got to wondering all over again: what was the deal? Every single house was decked, but still not theirs. Santa would not see them, would not leave gifts. Frederick spent the day chewing his nails ragged, asking to call Kelsey and being denied. His parents bundled him up for their annual visit to the church, where Frederick did not see Kelsey as he expected to, nor did he find baby Jesus, for the manger on the lawn stood empty, no footprints in the snow.

They just took him in before the snow came, Frederick told himself as the assembled congregation lifted their voices in song. He mumbled the words, looking again for Kelsey, and finding instead the sharp gaze of Mrs. Adams. She looked at him somewhat sadly, and he thought again of her boys—but he'd never seen her with boys, it didn't make sense.

Frederick allowed himself to be tucked into bed that night, tucked beyond all manner of reason, for he could not so much as turn over. His parents made no mention of Christmas, nor of Santa, and they locked his door when they closed it. *Locked!*

Sometime later, when Frederick had yet to fall asleep, he heard the knocking. He forcefully untucked himself, and crept to the window. The tapping came again, upon his windowpane. He threw back the sash and found Kelsey crouched there, a trail of footprints leading from the tree across the roof to his window.

"What in the heck—"

Kelsey covered his mouth with her hand. "The sleigh is up there—he's here," she whispered.

Frederick craned his neck, but could not see the next level of roof where the chimney was. Kelsey pulled him out the window and together they climbed up one more level, Frederick hardly noticing the snow on his bare feet because there was the sleigh, and there were the reindeer—only they weren't like he'd pictured. They were monsters, hulking and huge, their hides as black as night, their antlers reaching up into the stars. The reindeer looked at him and Kelsey with impassive, dark eyes, their fanged mouths hanging open to blow steam into the Christmas eve night.

"Uh," Frederick said.

"Down the chimney," Kelsey said.

Frederick had an image of Mrs. Adams's boys suddenly, wedged and suffocating in a chimney, but there he was, crawling inside the passage. He was perfectly suited to it, not too big and not too small. I'm just dreaming, he decided because like the missing Pine Street, it didn't make any sense, sliding down the flue, soot darkening his hands and pajamas.

He tumbled into the andirons and the charred wood and he helped soot-coated Kelsey climb down beside him. If this had been a nightmare, Frederick supposed the fire still would have been crackling, and they would have burned up, but this was a nonsense dream, so they sat on the andirons like logs, watching the living room beyond, where a man in a red suit was picking up a sack from the floor. It looked impossibly heavy, this sack, all lumpy and wet, but of course it had snowed and he'd come down from the roof.

The man turned to survey his work—there was no tree to leave presents under—and he sighed. It seemed good, whatever he saw. This man, caught in the light from the street slanting in the front window, looked like Frederick's grandfather—or rather, like Santa Claus, his hair grown long and white with a beard to match. He was dressed in red, but it was a wet kind of red. Frederick could see strands of stringed popcorn trailing from the mouth of his clumsy bag.

It occurred to Frederick that the man would need to leave via the chimney—and where were his parents, chastising him for not using the door, for leaving wet boot prints all over the floor and reindeer upon the roof of all places. Frederick's hand tightened on Kelsey's arm. It also occurred to Frederick that Kelsey lived with her grandmother, no parents at all since last year. Last year when...

"Santa is real," Federick whispered.

The man's attention swung to the fireplace and he crouched before them, his awkward bag making a *drip drip drip* behind him. His eyes were voids, wholly black and endless. *He sees me when I'm sleeping*, Frederick thought, and knew it to be true.

"You've been good," the man said, "for goodness sake." He put a finger across his lips. "Don't cry. Don't pout."

Kelsey pulled Frederick from the fireplace then, and far across the room, where they huddled until the man had wedged himself and his sack into the flue. And up they went, and up some more, until Frederick could hear the footsteps on the roof, and the the clatter as all those reindeer took into the sky. Snow filtered down across the dark night, blurring the lighted houses across the street.

Frederick left sooty footprints in his scamper across the room, Kelsey trailing behind. Up and up the staircase he flew, to his parents' bedroom where—Where—It was a wet kind of red.

"You have grandparents, right?" Kelsey asked behind him.

"Santa's not—Not real," Frederick sputtered. "Christmas isn't—"

"Isn't green," Kelsey whispered. "Only red."

Only red, Frederick thought, amazed how it wasn't horror that closed around his sight of all the red, but rather joy, at the idea of freedom, at the idea of knowing, of knowing once and for true, that Santa Claus was *real*. He couldn't wait to tell Taylor.

Deck Them All
Erica Barnes

"That's your tenth eggnog, dear," said Mrs. Claus. Her exhausted expression matched her monotonous tone. "Don't you think you should…slow down?"

"No." Jolly old Saint Nick hiccupped, adjusting his black sash. "I wanted to hit fifteen before takeoff."

She sighed. "You smell like you've had twenty."

"Perfect." He ignored her attempted insult and downed the rest of the thick liquid. Tinged with not only a soft sprinkle of cinnamon, but also a mere ass load of whiskey, Nick was ready for another bowl full.

The old couple made their way down the many hallways of the toy factory, toward the runway where the sleigh, reindeer, and far too many elves were waiting to send Nick off for the night with a merry farewell. He adjusted the velvet red cap atop his snow-white hair, pulled at the collar of the heavy jacket he wore, and checked the time on his golden pocket watch, engraved with his initials as a gift from the missus. On time, just like they had been for the past thousand or more years. They'd all been doing it so long that they had the schedule down to a schedule.

Hopefully the elves were finished packing all the sacks, the reindeer had taken a bathroom break or two…

"Nick…"

Did he need to take a bathroom break? No, he'd taken care of that earlier after a couple Yule logs. Did he check *every* name twice? Were all the names on the right list? He couldn't take another round of hearing *those* complaints again.

"Sweetheart…"

The reindeer stables had been upgraded. The elves quarters had been redecorated for morale. Oh god, had the sleigh gone through enough maintenance after last year's debacle?

"NICHOLAS!"

"WHAT?!" Nick snapped, glaring over at Mrs. Claus before he could catch himself.

Ah, shit.

She glared back at him. Then…she pinched those little lips of hers and faced straight ahead. "Nothing."

Great. She had him by the jingle bells for that one. After a long, deep breath, he tried again. "I'm sorry. What did you want to tell me?"

After a great deal of thinking it over, she finally loosened up. Before the words were even out of her mouth, though, he could guess what it was she wanted to talk about. "I was just going to ask if we could…you know…have a few moments together when you were finished tonight. Before we get into the rush of next year's Christmas? I feel like we don't get to spend time together anymore."

"*Darling*, we've talked about this. It's a long night, and I'm tired when I get back." They'd had this same conversation every year for…well…a long, long, *long* time. His eternal life had become one big feeling of déjà vu. Was there anything he couldn't predict down to the word or the second? "We'll see, okay?"

"I know what 'we'll see' means," she muttered, dropping the subject.

The two arrived at the runway to a deafening cheer, thousands of elves wearing smiles and jingling with every movement. The adoration in their eyes, the unshed tears…it was all too much. He didn't know if it was because of the tense silence between him and the missus, the fact that it was the exact same reaction the elves had year after year, or if it was because of the mounting stress he especially felt this Christmas. Whatever the reason, the decorations were all just too bright, the celebration was far too loud, and the reindeer smelled like they'd missed a few baths.

"Santa's here!"

"We've been waiting for so many minutes!"

"Weather's lookin' top notch out there! Clear skies til morning!"

Nick made his way through the crowd with Mrs. Claus, feeling the elves surround them as they got closer to the sleigh. The reindeer stomped in anticipation of the impending flight, huffing and jingling the bells on their collar. He couldn't wait for this damn night to be over with already and it hadn't even started.

Slinging a heavy black boot into the sleigh, one after the other, he got situated to where he was comfortable, then turned to face Mrs. Claus. He was surprised to find a travel mug extended toward him, steam rising from the opening.

"Hot cocoa to balance out all the eggnog," she said, handing him the mug. "With extra marshmallows."

He sniffed the drink and gave her a quizzical look. "Is it poisoned?"

Mrs. Claus huffed. "No, Nicholas, it's not poisoned."

"Well, then…thank you." Nick was at a loss for what to say. He still had a long night ahead. He didn't want this between them. "Listen—"

"Have a good night, Santa. See you in the morning," she told him sweetly, shuffling back so elves could slowly fill the space where she'd been standing.

Nick saw the sad expression on her face as she disappeared into the sea of green and red and gold. He sunk back into the sleigh, his disposition gloomier than before. All night long, that's all he would be able to think about now.

"On Dasher!" he exclaimed, grabbing the reins and looking out at the snowy environment before him. "On Dancer, on Prancer, on Vixen! On—"

He sighed. Screw it.

Giving the reins a whip, the reindeer took off in a run, and then slowly started to rise, lifting higher and higher into the night sky until they were above the clouds.

"Let's get this crap over with."

* * *

The stars twinkled as Nick flew at a leisurely pace over the world. While he only had one night, magic allowed time to flow differently as he went from house to house to deliver all the presents in time. No rushing, no one to pester him with questions, just him and the reindeer doing what they normally did. What they always did…year after year. He could probably do this with his eyes closed. So, why not do just that?

Nick leaned back in the sleigh and closed his eyes, taking in the silence, and the way the wind blew across his rosy cheeks. It was a rare respite from the joyful laughter, the grating songs that never ended.

It was almost—

"YIPEE!"

Nick jolted up out of his seat so fast, he almost jerked the reindeer into a panic. He turned with wide eyes to the back of the sleigh where the toy sacks sat. "Who the hell is back there?!"

"I'm so sorry! I'm so sorry!" came a high-pitched, squeaky voice.

Oh no.

He knew that voice.

From out of the biggest sack of toys popped a tiny little head, face covered in white powder. The bell at the tip of his hat jingled as he moved his head from left to right, eyes wide in panic while he tried to get his bearings straight. Nick groaned. It was too late to turn back now and return him to the North Pole.

"What are you doin' here, Tinsel?" Nick asked. "And why is that Snow Dust shit all over your face? There are kids toys in there."

He sniffed long and hard, wiping an arm across his face.

"I didn't know you'd left."

"There was a whole damn cheering section. How'd you miss that?"

"I was super focused, Santa!" Tinsel scrambled to the front, his little feet kicking until he tumbled into the open seat beside Nick. "There was a toy train that seemed to skip inspection. But *I* managed to catch that it appeared to be missing a wheel. Do you know how sad a child would have been to receive that toy?"

"Did you fix it?"

"It didn't need fixed," he said, taking another long sniff of the powder. "You found me when I'd just discovered that there had been four wheels all along. Crisis averted!"

Nick took a deep breath. And then another. Now he was stuck with this little snow devil the rest of the night. "Wonderful."

"So when do we start delivering presents?"

Sniff.

Nick frowned. "Soon. We're over Nevada now."

"I can help! I can help! I'm great at displaying presents!"

Snort.

"For crying out loud, Tinsel, quit takin' that crap!"

Tinsel stared wide-eyed at Nick, his snow globe shaped container full of Snow Dust gripped tight in his hand. "B-But Mr. Claus…it keeps me peppy! It's how I can keep track of all the details! And it's not just me!" Tinsel's eyes narrowed. "I can smell the eggnog on you."

"That is not the same as taking Dust from that shady snowman outside the workshop!"

"How did you—"

"I see you when you're sleeping, dumbass. I think I'll know when you're making bad deals with yellow snowmen!"

Tinsel's face reddened to match his shirt. "That's creepy!"

They were getting off topic, and Nick was on his final straw for the night. "Throw it away, Tinsel."

"Snickerdoodle spikes the work room punch."

"Throw it *away*, Tinsel."

"Carol steals all the candy canes. And it's *not* to eat them!"

"That's it!" Nick couldn't do it anymore.

He grabbed the container full of potent Snow Dust, and chucked it as hard as he could over the sleigh. There was only a brief silence while Tinsel registered what Nick had done. Then he leaned over the sleigh with a distraught expression.

"You fudgy batch of rotten cookies!"

Nick chuckled. That oughta teach him.

His laughter was cut short when Tinsel leaped out of the sleigh.

"You—" Nick growled, making sure to hold the reins as he glanced out over where Tinsel jumped. A bag of godforsaken Dust wasn't worth it.

Nick settled back in his seat. Tinsel had made his choice, and Nick wasn't going to go after him and clean up his mess.

Nope. He was going to enjoy the rest of his awful night in peace and quiet. He was going to just sit right here…as far away from that elf as he could get…

No one would know if he left him.

Not a soul!

Nick sighed and turned the reindeer around, diving down where Tinsel and the Snow Dust had fallen. The lower he went, the more he could see of the landscape below, all the twinkling lights laid out before him. Of course this would be where he'd have to search for the little drug-addled elf.

Las Vegas, here they come.

* * *

The Vegas strip grew bigger as the sleigh came in for a landing atop Vegas' Venetian hotel. The reindeer stumbled as they hit the rooftop, jarring Nick when the sleigh came to a stop. This night couldn't be over fast enough.

He used magic to hide the reindeer and sleigh from wandering eyes, and then, in a swirl of sparkles and winter wonder and all that shit, he transported to the street in the blink of an eye. According to his Santa Vision, Tinsel had run off to some backdoor gambling den. All Nick could see in the vision was smoke, cards, and skin.

Thankfully, there were about a million Santas roaming the decorated streets. The store santas, the dressed up dads, the santas ringing bells on the sidewalk. He blended in well, unnoticeable to everyone except the observant eyes of passing children. All they did was stare, much to the irritation of their parents, but nothing that incriminated him.

Not that anyone believes anyway, he thought. Everyone

had told so many stories about him over the years, that he had no reputation to hold on to, no identity to protect. If he told someone he was Papa Noel, they'd laugh at him or think he was crazy. If he told them he was looking for a strung out elf, they'd definitely sprint in the other direction.

Before he could enter the nondescript building he foresaw Tinsel at, there was a commotion from down the alleyway just beside it. Nick peeked around the corner to see an older man in tattered clothing with his back against a dumpster. In front of him were two larger men; lumbering closer to the poor guy with what could only be ill intent. Or so the baseball bat and knives in their hands said. The fire burning from a trash bin illuminated the lonely man's face. He was frightened.

The man was homeless, presumably. He had no weapon. Were these loan sharks coming to collect? Some people he'd pissed off coming to give him a scare? What the hell was their problem? What the actual hell was everyone's problem? Why was everyone so goddamn heartless these days? Who woke up one morning and said, 'You know, I think I'm going to make someone's life worse today.'

The whole, entire planet had lost their collective minds. No loving thy neighbor anymore because now people had to fear their neighbor. People couldn't leave anything unlocked; they couldn't walk down the street. If they fell down, if they got into trouble, everyone just whipped out a phone now or looked the other way. No one helped. No one cared.

I care, he thought. Try as he might not to anymore, he

did. He cared about a world full of people who were nothing but selfish pricks these days. Even the children who used to be the hope he had for the future were turning into little turds that screamed and shrieked for every little thing they didn't get. He knew he wasn't some saint…well, actually he was…but the whole world could do so much better. Maybe he needed to start doing better, too. From now on, maybe he would start being the change he wanted to see.

Except tonight.

Tonight was for self-care.

With steps as light as a feather, Nick snuck up behind the two imposing figures and banged their hard skulls together. The homeless man looked at him in a daze, and the two goons on the ground groaned in pain. Kicking the knife away, Nick grabbed the baseball bat and twirled it in his hand.

"Is that…Santa Claus?" one of the guys on the ground mumbled, holding a hand to the side of his bloodied head.

"Merry Christmas, shit stain."

Bang. A perfect hit to the nose. The first guy fell, hard.

Wham. An extra swing for good measure.

Clang. The second guy crumpled, holding his stomach where Nick struck.

Bam. Nick hit him. Again, and again, and again, the bat came down on the last guy's skull until there wasn't much skull left. And then Nick swung some more.

"BE. FUCKING. NICER."

Each word was punctuated with a strong hit, a lifetime's worth of pent up aggression. A desire to better the world, but unable to do anything but give out presents. Eliminating a couple of scumbags seemed like a decent gift to the world.

And oh holy night, it felt so right.

"Th-Thank you, mister," the old gentleman said. "I-I think."

"Take that," Nick said, kicking the knife toward the old man. "My Christmas gift to you."

The man quickly grabbed it and held it to his chest. "What do we do about them?"

"*We* do nothing. You're going to get as far away from here as you can get."

"What about you?"

Nick sighed and rested the bloody bat against his shoulder, walking toward the building he meant to go to in the first place. Except now, he was ready for whatever colorful crowd Tinsel had gotten tangled up with. "I'm going to get my elf back."

* * *

Inside, Nick walked through the crowd of people, ignoring the lingering gazes on his newest gear. Men went for the concealed weapons at their sides, while the scantily clad women looked unfazed or intrigued. They say never bring a knife to a gunfight, but those people weren't centuries old, either.

"Who the hell are you?" one guy asked.

"Oh my god, did someone order a Santa for the night?" one of the blonde women asked with a bright smile. "Is he gonna strip for us? Do a little jiggle, baby!"

"I'm looking for Tinsel," Nick announced so the whole

room would hear. Everyone fell silent. "I know he's here somewhere, so someone tell me how to get to him."

"We ain't telling you shit, old man," the guy from earlier said. He looked young and full of stupidity. "Now, if you haven't been invited to this here shindig, I'm afraid you're gonna have to take your ancient ass elsewhere."

"Well that's not happening. So tell me where the little Snow blower is, and I'll be out of your hair."

He pulled a pistol out and pointed it at Nick. "I said it's time to get the hell out."

There was no hesitation when Nick took the bat and swung at the guy's head. He was out cold on the floor, and now everyone was screaming. He was going to wring Tinsel's neck for all the extra chaos he had to go through tonight.

"And I said I want to find my damn elf. Now...where is he?!"

Multiple guns were trained on Nick, ranging from more pistols to shotguns. When they all fired around the same time, Nick touched his nose and gave it a little wiggle. Every bullet in the place froze mid-air, then dropped with the most satisfying *clink*. The look of fright and panic on everyone's faces was worth the magic trick.

Nick grabbed an empty beer bottle, broke it in half over a pool table, and stabbed it into the first throat he could find from one of the many assholes in the room that'd shot at him. All hell broke loose after that, and everyone but the screaming women were headed right for Nick.

Breaking a pool stick in half, he killed two jackasses with

one stone, stabbing them through the chest. He then proceeded to pick up someone's pistol and unload the rest of the magazine on as many people as he could hit. The women curled up in a corner, shaking in terror at the bloody massacre. Nick was past worrying about them. They'd made their poor choice in company. They could hide in fear the rest of the night and make his life easier.

Still…a pang of guilt passed through him. It was their Christmas Eve too.

There was one bastard left in the room, cut up and limping for the exit. Nick grabbed a hold of him and let loose with his gloved fists, giving blow after blow. Finally, woozy and disoriented, the man pointed at a back door.

"There…the elf's back there. He's with Ginger."

Nick grunted in response and gave the man one last, forceful punch.

With slow, heavy steps, he walked over the dead bodies littering the dingy floor and went to the door the man pointed out. Trusty baseball bat at the ready, Nick opened the door carefully; unsure of what would be on the other side. Unfortunately, it was everything he'd feared.

Tinsel was wrapped up in some red head's arms, sniffing lines of Snow Dust off places Nick didn't want to see from anyone but his wife. He turned in disgust, upset in his Santa Vision for not giving him a heads up on this one. What the hell was this night turning into?

"Get your tiny hands off that woman and come on!" Nick bellowed. "I have had one hell of a night, and I do not want to deal with you now too."

Tinsel about snorted and choked on the line he was doing. Nick wasn't that lucky, though. And he couldn't bring himself to give Tinsel the same fate he'd given the others.

"Santa!" Tinsel shouted, seemingly not sure whether to be more surprised by Nick being there, or his appearance. "I…I'm not…*please don't make me leave.* I don't want to lose my Dust, or my girl, or—"

"Listen here, you little nightmare," Santa said, finger pointed right at Tinsel. "You can keep your Snow Dust for now. You can even keep your lady friend here. But you will get on that sleigh, and you will help me make the rest of my deliveries tonight. And when we get back home, you will throw that garbage out and get some fucking help. Do you understand me?"

"Yes, sir," Tinsel said, meek and ashamed. He turned to the taller woman beside him. "What do you say? Wanna…go for a ride?"

"With you?" She smiled, flicking the bell on his hat as she pulled a gingerbread designed silk robe on. "Absolutely."

"Great," Nick deadpanned. "Now let's go deliver these presents and end this horror show."

The three of them began to walk out when Tinsel piped up. "Um…Santa?"

"What?"

"Why are you so…bloody?"

For maybe the first time that night, Nick smiled. "Why don't I show you?"

* * *

This Christmas Eve was like no other Christmas Eve. As a

man who'd experienced the same routine day in and day out, all delivery nights being the exact same as the last, this one was…different. Special.

Whatever he'd started that night hadn't stopped. There was a certain carefree nature to him, the tightness in his chest now loosened. He cared, and yet, he didn't care. The atrocities he saw in Vegas weren't the last. The terrors he created there weren't the last either. All throughout the world, and all through the night, old Kris Kringle no longer held back.

When he saw a scared little girl hiding in her house because her drunk relative hurt her, Nick made sure the relative didn't hurt her again thanks to a rather large rolling pin. When an elderly woman fell in the park, and a group of passerby started laughing, Nick silenced their laughs with an old pipe to a few heads and kneecaps. And when a young couple was tailed by a group of strangers looking to do harm, Nick was the one who harmed first. Strangely, the pairs of skis he pulled from his toy sack turned out to be extremely useful.

Tonight, no one would be scared on Christmas Eve. Tonight, he'd make sure people remembered to be kind and respectful to one another. Tinsel still wasn't quite sure what to do or say about Nick's newest hobby, but he astutely decided to say nothing. Instead, he stuck mostly to sucking face with his new friend in the back of the sleigh.

By the end of the night, Santa's suit was a new shade of red, his body was sore, and his heart was…full. Nick couldn't remember the last time he'd enjoyed a Christmas

Eve night. The delivery had gone by quickly, and he didn't feel so…so trapped. When they got back to the North Pole, the northern lights danced across the sky. It brought with it a sense of peace for the old toymaker.

When the sleigh was parked, and all the other elves cheered for Nick's return—and only slightly questioned Tinsel's acquaintance with a full grown woman, or Nick's bloody accessories—there was one place Nick had been waiting to get back to all night. He went inside, and straight for his room, leaving the rest of the elves to celebrate yet another successful Christmas Eve.

Nick opened the door to his bedroom and was pleased to see the lamp still on. There in her rocker was Mrs. Claus, as beautiful as ever. She looked up at Nick's entrance, a smile forming before she seemed to remember that they'd left on a sourer note. Nick, however, wasn't going to let that stop him.

With a quick stride to where she was, he picked Mrs. Claus up in one smooth motion and carried her to the bed. Gently, he laid her down, and then hopped onto the bed beside her. Mrs. Claus fell into a fit of laughter as she eyed Nick up and down. "What's gotten into you?"

"I don't know, but I know what I'd like to get into," he said seductively.

"Oh," she said, pretending to sound appalled. "I'm being serious. Did you have a good night? Did everything go as planned?"

Nick thought the question over. For the first time in centuries, he was happy to say that it hadn't gone as planned. For once, he hadn't known what was going to happen next, and he hadn't hated every minute of the entire trip.

"There were a few bumps, but…I actually had a good night." He brushed a strand of gray hair from her face. She didn't need to know about the new dye job for the Santa suit yet. "More than that, I wanted to get back to my favorite gift of all."

"Well, aren't you charming tonight." Mrs. Claus grinned and leaned in to Nick to give him a comforting hug. "I'm glad to see you back, though."

"I'm glad to be back. I think I owe you a little one-on-one time, too."

A hesitant smile brightened Mrs. Claus' face. "Do you mean it? You're not tired?"

"Of course I mean it." He meant it when he wanted to be the change. Which meant he needed to be the husband his wife deserved. The world was an awful enough place. Treating the ones he cared about like he actually cared about them was the least he could do to make it a better place.

"Oh, Nicholas," she said, draping her arms around him to give him a hug.

"Besides," he said, thinking over the bizarre night. The relief, the release, and the thrill of doing something that he hadn't done year after year. Maybe, just maybe, this was his way to break the curse of monotony. Maybe this was his way of making the better world he wanted. "I think it's about time we started some new traditions."

Naughty
Justin Hunter

I land at the bottom of the chimney and squeeze out into the living room. A few presents are tucked under my arm and I toss them at the tree. They land expertly and arrange themselves, nestling in the perfect places under the boughs. I should be gone already. Hell, I usually just toss the fucking presents down the chimney and let them do all the work themselves. I don't even have to leave my sleigh if I don't want too and I usually fucking don't. I've been doing this shit for a couple hundred years now and could do it in my sleep. Except, for some reason I was actually paying attention and saw some guy coming in here through a window. The dude doesn't live here. How do I know this? I'm Santa. I fucking know everybody and their addresses and if they're getting a visit from me. The kid that lives here is on my nice list and I don't want this guy fucking up his Christmas.

I don't hear the guy and a quick glance around tells me nothing. There's a slight breeze from the window he left open. The guy must be hiding and I know it's my fault because I do make a good amount of noise zipping down the chimney and all.

"Santa?"

I look up toward the top of the stairs and see the kid looking at me. I must have been louder than I thought.

"Ho! Ho! Ho!" I say. I can't help it. Kids get me all a-Ho-ing. I love those little fuckers. "What are you doing awake? Didn't your parents tell you that Santa only comes when you are asleep?"

"I was sleeping, Santa," the kid says. "I woke up when I heard a crash." He points and I look over to see a vase knocked off a side table near the open window.

"Did you do that?" the kid says.

"I didn't," I say. "Santa is as light on his feet as a feather! Vases stay in their places when I tip-toe about!" I wince inwardly. Why do I talk like this when speaking to kids? I sound like an idiot.

"My mom is going to be mad," the kid says. "She bought that vase for grandma and grandma gave it back to her on my mom's birthday. She forgot that my mom gave it to her. So my mom used that to tell a lawyer that my grandma was losing her mind and couldn't take care of herself anymore. Now my grandma is in a nursing home and my mom doesn't have to go over to her house and clean it up on the weekend or bring her food anymore or anything like that. She calls it her freedom vase."

"Wow," I say. "Your mom sounds great."

"I've been very good this year."

"That's why I'm here," I say.

"When did you put me on the nice list?"

"When Suzie Jenkins dropped her papers at school, you helped her pick them up," I say. "That tipped the scales in your favor."

"I only helped her because I wanted you to put me on the nice list," he says.

"Well," I say. "That's okay. I'm more about the resulting actions than the motivation behind the choices. Also, your frontal cortex won't be fully developed until you're twenty-five or so. Santa can't count on little guys like you to have proper executive functioning." The kid looks a little confused and then points to a little plate of treats by the fireplace.

"Didn't you eat my cookies?" the kid says, "I left those for you."

"Ho! Ho! Ho! No," I say.

"Why not?"

"Santa doesn't want to get diabetes," I say, wondering why Santa always seems to speak in the third person. "It runs in Santa's family."

"What's diabetes?"

"Don't worry about it," I say. "Now what presents do you want Santa to put under the tree?"

"You don't like my cookies?" The kid says, looking like he's about to cry.

"Not at all!" I say, reaching out and giving him a reassuring pat on the shoulder. "I love cookies and I can tell how much effort you put into making these! Wow!" My jaw hurts from feigning so much enthusiasm. I pick up the plastic plate. There's four cookies on it. They tower with frosting. Bits of various candies and sprinkles fall off of them.

"Can you take just one bite?" The kid says.

"Can you tell Santa if you washed your hands before making these?" I say. I think I see a bit of dried mucus under the kid's nose. He wiped that with his sleeve for sure. I look at the cookies as if they're crawling with maggots.

"I washed."

"Santa's not sure if he believes you."

"Well," The kid says. "I took a bath last night."

"Wonderful…" I pick up a cookie and take a bite. My teeth sink into frosting and hit a hidden chunk of peppermint hard candy.

"Do you like it?" The kid says.

"This is magical," I say, chewing hard. I put the plate back down on the ground near the fireplace.

"You don't want more?"

"Santa has millions of kids to see. That's a lot of cookies. I need to save room in my belly." I put a hand on my gut and jiggle up and down. He laughs.

"You have a big tummy!"

"Santa doesn't take very good care of himself," I say. "He has a problem with portion control. Can you tell me something, little boy? Did one of Santa's helpers come in here a little before me? I think he came through the window."

"He's in the bathroom," the kid says, pointing to a closed door down the hallway. "Is he an elf? He's much too big to be an elf. In the old TV shows the elves are very small."

"Elves come in all shapes and sizes," I say. "I feed them much better than I used too."

"He was wearing clothes like my daddy has," the kid says.

"Elves are very brand-conscious," I say. "Hey, speaking of your daddy, are your parents here?"

"They went to the casino," he says. "They go every Friday night. They say I can't leave the house or use the stove while they are gone."

"Good to know," I say. "What wonderful caregivers! Say, why don't you go upstairs for a bit? I have to give you your presents and have a little talk with my elf."

"I want to see my presents!"

"You'll spoil the surprise," I say. "Naughty boys who peek at their presents before Christmas get bad magic. Their gifts turn into coal!"

"No!"

"Yes! Off you pop!" I say. The kid runs upstairs. I grab the fireplace poker. I wait just a bit to make sure I don't hear the kid moving around upstairs and head toward the bathroom door. I step lightly, but the fucking floor squeaks like a bastard. There's nothing to be heard from behind the door. I knock. No answer.

"Come on out," I say in a whisper. "Leave by the front door. No cops. You go home and I go back to doing my job." The door opens and a man steps into the hallway. He's taller than me. A knife is clasped in his hand. I point the fire poker at him.

"You are a bad boy," I say.

"I'm going to open you up from cock to sternum," he says.

"Imagine little Kimble Mackintosh pulling a knife on

Santa," I say. "What would your mother think?" The knife in his hand drops a bit lower.

"How the fuck do you know who I am?"

"Santa knows the names of all the children in the world," I say. "It's not your fault you were named 'Kim'. Your parents should have known the other children would make fun of you and turn you into a real bastard."

"It's Joakim," he says. "Not Kim."

"But everyone called you Kim."

"It's a unisex name!"

"I know that," I say. "I'm Santa. I know all about names. Hell, it means War God in the Welsh language and has vaunted Hebrew origins. Kings were named Kim."

"I know!" He says. The knife was down at his side now. The arm holding it hanging limply. "I tried telling the other kids that! They didn't listen!"

"They didn't listen," I say. "Middle school can be so hard."

"The name is so feminized in America," He says. "I don't know what my parents were thinking!"

I cracked him across the face with the fire poker. He fell back into the hallway. I moved forward, stilling swinging away, hitting him wherever I could.

"Just because (whack!) your parents (whack!) named you Kim (whack!) doesn't mean (whack!) you get to be (whack!) a little shit (whack!) and steal candy bars (whack!) from the drugstore (whack!) with money that (whack!) was supposed to (whack!) be put in the (whack!) offering plate (whack!) at church!"

Kim lay in the hallway bleeding and breathing hard. I heard running from upstairs.

"KID," I said, "IF YOU DON'T GO BACK TO BED YOU'RE NOT GETTING ANY CHRISTMAS PRESENTS FOR THE NEXT DECADE!" I heard the footsteps run back and a door close. "SANTA ISN'T MAD AT YOU! I'M JUST HAVING A LITTLE WORK DISCUSSION DOWN HERE WITH MY ELF! YOU ARE ON MY GOOD LIST! JUST STAY IN YOUR ROOM! SANTA LOVES YOU!"

I felt a hard punch in my stomach. I felt a long blade nick my spine and then was pulled off my feet from an upward yank of the blade. Kim ripped the knife from me. I fell back against the wall. The poker dropping from my grasp, I put my hands over my stomach. Ropes of intestines began slipping through my fingers as I tried to keep my insides inside. I looked up at Kim. The knife-holding arm was covered in my blood up to the elbow.

"That's why I didn't get any presents back in '94?" Kim said. "Because I stole candy from the drugstore a few times? That's all it took?"

"I give the presents," I said. "I make the rules." I began shoving intestines back into my stomach. "Would you go find me some duct tape?"

"What about the kids that bullied me because of my name? Did they get presents that year? What about Nate Smyth? The kid who put my backpack in the urinal at school and pissed on it. What about Patrick Lee? He kicked me in the nuts every day for two weeks after gym class until the teacher made him stop. What about them?"

"The good list," I said. Kim stepped forward and stabbed me in the chest. The knife slipped in and out like silk.

"The fucking good list?" he said. "Those animals?"

"You don't understand," I said.

"Make me understand!" Kim said, stepping forward, he stabbed at me again. I grabbed his wrist with one hand and snapped it like a twig. The knife fell. He began screaming, which only made it easier to knock six of his teeth out with a head butt. I kicked him in the balls and he fell, rolling onto his stomach. I knelt on him, wrapping my intestines around his neck. The fuckers were too slippery to get a good choke going, but I did what I could without tearing myself up too bad.

"Understand this," I said. "You can *not* hurt Santa Claus. I'm fucking immortal. You know how many times I've been shot, blown up, electrocuted, or set afire? You think people don't lay in wait for me every year waiting to take a shot at ol' Kris Kringle? You try delivering presents to the good little children of Syria. It ain't fucking easy. If I say you're naughty, then you better well believe that you are. I see you when you're fucking sleeping. I know when you're fucking awake. I know if you've been bad or good. So fuck you!"

Kim was gasping for air. His mouth was working so I let up on the choke a bit to hear him.

"Just...candy...bars."

"Just candy bars," I said. "You don't know a fucking thing, Kimbo. That drugstore was run part time by a fourteen-year-old kid named Morty Loganstern. His parents owned the shop. He couldn't do any of the pharmacy stuff, but he could take over the register if his parents needed a break for a bit. That kid worked harder in a week than most kids his age do all year. You remember him?"

"All…fucked…up…kid."

"Yeah," I say. "His face got all burned up in a fire when he was just a baby. You think you got bullied bad back in the day, he couldn't even go to school at all it was so bad. Anyway, Morty's parents did an inventory check once a week and they noticed all the missing candy bars. You took so fucking many, Kim, what the fuck?"

"I'm…sorry."

"It doesn't matter," I say. "They blamed him for the missing candy. No working cameras in the place. They got so fed up with him that they grounded him from working the register. He got so upset that night he actually did steal something from the drugstore. He thought that if he was going to be blamed for stealing that he might as well actually do it. He took a quart of whiskey and a pack of smokes. That night he got drunk behind what was an old nursing home down Roosevelt Street across highway 34. Remember that place?"

"No."

"You wouldn't," I say. "He tossed a cigarette into the bushes behind that building and wandered off. He didn't mean for it to happen but the bush caught fire and burned which burned the nursing home down. It was a shitty place. Cost cutting owners. Smoke alarms didn't work. The place was too lit before they could get the people out. Three hundred people died. When Morty heard about what happened, he killed himself by jumping off the 34 bridge the very next day. Those simple candy bars you stole ended up killing so many people and ruining families. It was like an atomic bomb of grief and suffering."

"I…didn't…know," he says. I lean in close, tightening the grip on my intestines to gut-choke the fucker.

"Naughty list," I say and twist and pull. His neck stretches. Vertebrae pop. He dies. I drag Kim's body over to the chimney, letting my guts fall all over the place as I go. I touch the side of my nose. There's a twinkle and the body shoots up the flu like a rocket. I hear a whoosh and a crash as the body crashes through the chimney cap. He'll reach a thousand miles an hour pretty soon. Straight up. No brakes on this ride. I know that nobody's going to find Kim's body unless he bumps into a space shuttle. I stand up and turn around. The kid's standing at the top of the stairs. His mouth is open. His eyes wide with, not fear exactly, but at the very least shock. I spread my arms to him.

"Ho! Ho! Ho!" I say, I forgot about my entrails and something probably important thuds wetly to the floor from my rent gut. "Oops! Sorry about that. Santa had a bit of an accident."

"Are you hurt?" The kid says.

"Not Santa," I say, reaching down and picking up internal things that have fallen out—the usual red or purple bits and bobs—and sticking them back inside wherever they fit. I grab at my intestines and wind them as best as I can back in, but they don't want to sit right. "Santa is made of starlight, unicorn horns, and angel dust. I can't be hurt."

"What are those?" The kid says, pointing at my intestines.

"Those are Santa's sleigh reins. I keep them in my stomach. In case the reindeer break the ones I put on at the north pole."

"Is that blood?"

"Not at all, but I have to ask," I say. "Was there any dairy products in those cookies?"

"I think so. I used some milk."

"Santa threw up a little bit," I say. "I'm lactose intolerant."

"A little bit?" The kid says, looking around the downstairs. There's blood everywhere. "I'm sorry, Santa."

"Don't mention it," I say, "Just remember it for next year. Do you have any duct tape?"

"My dad has some in the garage."

"Ho! Ho! Ho! Go get it." The kid scrambles away, leaping over the bloody patches on the floor and comes back in a minute with a roll of tape. I jam the intestines back inside my stomach the best I can and wind the tape around myself until the whole roll is used up.

"Thank you," I say. "My, oh my, you are a very good boy. Go on back to bed now. It's almost Christmas morning."

"Okay, Santa," the kid says. He runs up the steps but stops at the top and looks back at me. "Can you please tell me one of my presents? Please?"

"Alright," I say. "You've been such a good boy. I got you a football and an RC car." The kid frowns.

"What about the PlayStation?"

"Santa isn't made of money, kid. You're getting an Intellivision."

"What's that?"

"An old gaming system," I say. "Your dad was feeling nostalgic when he bought it. He thinks you'll love it and he's looking forward to playing with you."

"Will I love it?"

"No," I say. "It sucks."

"Crap," the kid says, "Oh, Well. Goodbye, Santa."

"Goodbye kid," I say. "Remember I see you when you're sleeping. I know when you're awake."

"That's kind of creepy."

"Yup."

The kid goes to bed and I head on over to the chimney. I can't fucking believe how long this took. I should be in fucking Scotland by now. I check the tape one more time and then touch the side of my nose. There's a twinkle in my eye and off I go!

Jingle Hell
Leon Peter Blanda

For the most wonderful moment, I thought I was dead. But I'm not; I'm breathing.

The stench of singed hair tickled my nose. Smoke burned my eyes, curling up from the small fires voraciously chewing my beard away. I smacked out the flames, and the smoldering embers in my unkempt facial hair gave the dreadlocked clusters the appearance of cheap, half-smoked cigars.

My mind is as scattered as ornaments on a Christmas tree, and I'm having difficulty shuffling through the series of events that brought me here.

With great effort, I rolled onto my side. Every muscle is cramped, or completely numb. Drawing a deep breath, the absolute carnage unfolded before my itchy, tearful eyes.

Our house is more fire than framework, as is my workshop, and—dear Lord… The elves! Where are all the elves?

Charred aromas, the smell of overcooked meat, stung my nostrils seconds before I noticed the chunks of blackened, elven flesh and bones hanging from the evergreens, all covered with snow.

"Nick." A pained voice cried out, straining from

somewhere behind me.

Less than ten yards away, my beloved wife lies motionless. Gone are her apple-red curls, singed to the roots of her still-smoking scalp, scorched black. Where once was a plump, rosy cheek, torn flesh exposes a bloodied cheekbone to the night air, and broken, yellow teeth chatter with every ragged, dying breath.

The stretch of snow between us is as red as the bracts of a Poinsettia, and littered with the tiny, seared body parts of our adopted family. A half-dozen elf arms, with delicate, outstretched fingers, grow from the crimson snow, a gruesome flower bed of child-sized hands. Hanging over a branch on a snow-caked birch tree like wet laundry on a clothesline, is a pair of short legs, still wearing pointed wooden shoes, dripping blood so thick and dark it looks more like burnt motor oil. The rest of him was scattered in seared chunks throughout the frozen roots below.

Pointed ears and silver bells, caked with blood, shimmered in the trees and bushes. Gory ornaments on this unholy night.

"Nick," her voice was weaker this time, no louder than the smacking of chapped lips. A dying whisper. Nothing like the sweet songbird tone of the woman who sings Christmas carols all year round.

"I'm coming, Connie. Hold on!"

Scrambling under the burning sky, I fell to my knees beside her twisted body. Her breathing was shallow, labored. What I had not noticed before, and something I'll never forget for the rest of my unnatural life: her eyes. Her beautiful green eyes were gone, melted away, and drooling from the sockets, rolling down her cheeks like gooey, black eyeliner. The dark gore froze before falling from her face and looked more like dirty candlewax than the boiled remains of whatever composes the inside of an eyeball.

"Connie, I'm here," I said, softly. Lifting her head into my lap, the fetid stew weeping from her empty eye sockets stained the leg of my pants.

"Nick," she pleaded with half a breath.

"Don't speak. I'm here, jingle bell. Everything's going to be okay." I lied to my dying wife for the first time in our marriage.

"I can't sss—" she coughs, and her blood freckles the bridge of my nose and cheeks. "I can't see you, Nick. What's happening?"

It takes every ounce of magic left in me not to combust into tears.

A guttural croak crawls from her throat, followed by a geyser of dark sludge oozing between her exposed teeth, and seeping out of the hole in her cheek, dribbling down her chin like blackberry jam.

"CONNIE!" I would give her every pint of immortal blood in my veins, but that is a gift I can't give. I am not a vampire, and have never wanted to be one before this Christmas Eve.

The day I always feared has come, and I will soon be cursed to live the rest of eternity without her. We always knew it would happen someday—her being mortal and all—but neither of us could've guessed it would end like this.

"Nick," her voice is thin and raspy. "You have to—" she choked on her words. More blackberry sludge spills from her lips and the gash in her face.

"It's okay, jingle bell. I'm right here. I'm not going anywhere." I cradled her this one last time, as she convulsed in agony.

Connie squeezed my hand, then went limp. Her hand fell away before I noticed something dry and crumbled in my palm.

"Take it," she coughed.

"No. I don't want to be here anymore," my voice cracked. "I want to go with you."

"You can't," she whispered, and exhaled a breathy rasp. Blinking her eyes, Connie gazed off, looking past me, into the world beyond ours, into the Foreverafter. Then she was gone.

I mashed my face to hers one last time, kissing her cold, bloody lips. I kissed where our foreheads had just been pressed together, and gently rested her head in the soft snow. I'll have to come back to bury her.

Resting in my palm were the dry crumbs of a frosted sugar cookie. Once the shape of a Christmas tree, now it resembled everything else in my world: broken, destroyed. I scarfed the crumbled cookie in one bite—chewing felt like a luxury I could no longer afford—and immediately felt its effects. My legs no longer hurt. The singed parts of my beard began to grow out like time-lapse photography of a flower in bloom.

With the burst of physical rejuvenation returned my

scattered memory.

Precious moments ago, we stood on the porch of our home as a blended family: my wife and I, the elves, and elvlings… all of us hugging, holding hands, and whispering our tearful goodbyes.

We clung to each other in horror as the bright lights of many afterburners crested overhead. Rockets scorched the sky over the Northern Lights. Fireballs flew overhead, like dragons, with tails made of black smoke, connecting all the continents of the world with Romanesque arches of billowing smoke.

I remember thinking about all the good children of the world. The ones who were still awake, and who still believed in me—the ones who happened to be gazing up at the same brilliant balls of light soaring though the twinkling night sky—I wondered how many of them thought those nuclear payloads were me. I wonder how many children thought they were watching my sleigh streak across the sky. How many believed the impending doom was jolly ol' St. Nick on the way to deliver whatever gift they'd asked for… the one thing for which they had been good all year to earn?

My head still throbbed from the concussive wave of fire that killed the elves, and my dear wife. But my muscles no longer ached, and my beard was once again as white as the ash that rained from the heavens.

I ran to the stables, but as soon as I reached for the handle on the enormous, sliding barn doors, the roof collapsed. Before I heard the *KATHOOM!* of the explosion, the heavy doors fulminated off the rails, and knocked me back thirty yards. My boots dug long trenches in the fresh powder, but I managed to stay off my ass.

"Dasher! Dancer! Prancer! Vixen!" I screamed my throat raw. "Comet! Cupid! Donner! Blitzen!" The flames quickly wrestled the entire structure to its foundation, and the screaming cries of the dying reindeer were buried beneath the roaring, crackling conflagration, until choked out of existence.

Back on my feet, the weight of loss hangs heavy.

I turn, and a sparkle of hope shimmers in the near distance.

Miraculously, the toolshed behind the hill stood untouched. We call it a toolshed because we keep the tools in there, but it's more of a big garage. The toolshed was protected on all sides by the snowy knoll, and a thicket of old birch trees and sturdy arctic willows—which did not fair quite as well. Snow shaken from their blazing branches, the mighty trees burned like giant candles; the snow before them reflected brightly their flickering, warm, golden light.

I trudged up the hill as fast as I could, the freshly fallen snow and ash made it as impossible a task as running from a monster in a nightmare.

Inside the toolshed, my trusty, old sleigh sits untouched. Even after all these millennia, the lacquer is still shiny; everywhere except where I sit, and in two, small spots on the curled bow of the old boat where the leather reins have rubbed it away to bare wood. The sleigh sits heavy on its runners, packed to the brim with enormous, velveteen bags, overflowing with gifts that were intended to be delivered tonight. Bicycles, skateboards, video game systems, balls, bats, dolls, cats—stuffed and real—poke out from the cinched tops of the overstuffed, velvet duffels.

As I wonder what my next move should be, something growls behind me, and I freeze.

I raise my arms slowly, to show I'm unarmed. Before I can turn to see what has crept from the shadows to devour me, something big and wet slaps across my left cheek, hard, like being smacked across the face with a raw, pork tenderloin. The wet mass drags slimy, putrid stench up the side of my face. Fetid goo drips from my bushy eyebrow and rolls off my button nose, same as the thick drool rolling off the tip of the meaty tongue that just gave me the unwanted facial.

"Ho-Ho-Holy shit," I said, and my heart grew three sizes. Or maybe that's the sugar cookie working its magic.

"I forgot all about you," I said, running my fingers up the fuzzy jaw of the wretched beast. His breath smells worse than his dung, but I'm still glad to see him. "I guess we all do. Huh, buddy?"

Reindeers are gigantic, majestic creatures. Usually. As far as reindeers go, this one standing knock-kneed before me is…unfortunate—that's a nice word for it. Besides the malformed, glowing growth on his gaunt face, he's too skinny, all ribs and cockeyed antlers. One of his eyes is cloudy and pale, and his teeth are bucked further than I've ever seen on anything ever, including that Easter-lovin' hare.

I completely forgot about him in all the chaos. After having his humming nose broken several times, and being stabbed by someone's antlers during what Comet and Vixen called "reindeer games"—I removed Rudolf from the stables and set him up in the toolshed with the sleigh. It was the only way I could ensure the other reindeers wouldn't kill him.

My strength is growing, but I'm still weak. I can feel the sugar cookie surging through my veins, replenishing what keeps me alive, but I'll need more. A dozen or so to get back to full strength. Milk, too. Preferably whole.

There are advantages to being an unkillable myth that exists in the hearts and minds of children. It's funny; they are the most powerful creatures in the universe, children, until they hit about fourteen, fifteen. After that, it's, *"Bye-bye, imagination… Hello, hormones."*

"Give me a hand, Rudy," I pat the ugly beast between the eyes.

Together, we lighten the sleigh's load, removing the toy sacks, and tossing them aside in a pile. With my inhuman strength, I'm able to lift two, hefty sacks at a time; while Rudolf struggles to get his malformed, jagged antlers to catch onto the braided ropes cinching the bags shut.

Raaarrr! A live cat fusses from somewhere in the growing pile of overstuffed, velvet sacks as they smash on top of each other, but there's no time to sort through them all and find out which ones have cats inside and which ones don't. Besides, cats are good at finding their way out of sticky situations. I doubt there's a cat on Earth that will be put out by the apocalypse the rest of the world now faces. They're like furry cockroaches that way.

The ugly reindeer grunts and honks.

"I know. I know. But if it's only going to be you pulling the sleigh alone—we have to lighten the load, and ditch all this damn crap."

Rudolf brays.

"Sorry. Not crap. *Gifts*. We have to ditch all these damn *gifts*. There—ya happy?" I said, and totally understand why everybody gets annoyed with him. As far as reindeer go, Rudolf's not the most fun of the bunch.

Clopping his hooves, he nuzzled his head between my belly and my beard.

"Okay. Okay. Easy, boy." I rubbed the scruff under his chin, "Listen, buddy. Some real bad shit just went down. It looks like it's just you and me left… Maybe in the whole world."

Rudolf looks down at the loose hay scattered across the wooden floorboards. You can always tell when a reindeer is sad.

"Hey," I lifted his furry chin so that his eyes met mine, "You've got this, kiddo. I need you to guide my sleigh tonight. Now, give me one second."

I leave the reindeer, and run over to the toppling pile of enormous, velvet sacks. I toss open sashes, and dig through several, tossing toys asunder until I find what I'm looking for—

"Aha! Bingo." Clutched in my gloved hand, a Desert Eagle 50, intended to be delivered to a kid named Paul who pulled up his *C* to an *A* in Biology. What kind of idiot parent promises their kid a gun for getting good grades? A bad one, that's what kind. Whatever… I don't have time to update the Naughty List.

Racking the slide on the pistol feels good, reminds me of when I was a much younger man, before all the toys, and the elves, and… Connie. The instantly recognizable click-clack of the pistol chambering a round startles Rudolf.

"Don't worry, boy. This ain't for you," I chuckled, and sat down in the worn part of the bench behind the curled lip at the bow of the sleigh, cold steel in one hand, leather reins in the other. "This is for the sonuvabitch that just started World War III."

With the flick of my wrist, I snapped the reins, and Rudolf hurtled his body into the air, dragging the sleigh and my fat ass behind him. He crashed through the roof of the toolshed with his crooked antlers, and we soared into the burnt sky, bursting through the Roman pillars of rocket clouds.

Santa Claus is coming to town, and Hell's coming with me!

The Candy Caners

Multiple term past President of the Short Mystery Fiction Society, **Kevin R. Tipple** reviews books and short stories, watches way too much television, and offers unsolicited opinions on anything. His short fiction has appeared in magazines such as *Lynx Eye*, *Starblade*, *Show and Tell*, and *The Writer's Post Journal*, among others. *Mystery Weekly Magazine* published his story, The Damn Rodents Are Everywhere, in May of 2021 and soon had to change their name to *Mystery Magazine*. His short story, The Beetle's Last Fifty Grand, appears in the 2022 anthology, *Back Road Bobby and His Friends*, and everyone involved seems to have survived the experience unscathed. His short story, Visions of Reality, appears in *Crimeucopia-Say It Again*. Earlier this year, the *Notorious in North Texas: Metroplex Mysteries Volume III* anthology was released and includes his short story, Whatever Happened To…? Also released earlier this year is the anthology, *Larceny & Last Chances: 22 Stories of Mystery & Suspense*, which includes his crime fiction short story, The Hospital Boomerang. Fully trained before marriage, Kevin can work all major appliances and, despite a love of nearly all sports, is able to clean up after himself.

Alexander Bayliss lives with his family on the south coast of England. His work blends horror with historical fiction and detective writing. He is the author of *Jekyll & Hyde: Resurrection*, a sequel to Robert Louis Stevenson's gothic horror masterpiece. A mash-up of horror story and police procedural, it has been described as an 'ode to a classic' and a 'great read'. Alexander has also contributed to the acclaimed A-Z of Horror series of anthologies.

KM Rockwood draws on a varied background for her stories, including as a special education teacher in inner city and alternative schools. In addition, she has worked as a laborer in manufacturing facilities and supervised an inmate work crew in a large state prison. She is currently retired. Published works include the Jesse Damon Crime Novel series (Wildside) and numerous short stories.

Dante Bilec is an emerging Canadian writer of fantasy and horror fiction whose work has appeared in *Mobius Blvd* and *The Anthology of Horror*. He has a passion for classic horror radio dramas, foreign languages, the films of Dario Argento, and the lyrical poetry of Biggie Smalls and Marshall Mathers. Unironically, he hopes one day to be dissed on an Eminem record. Dante is currently working on his debut novel. He lives in Ontario, Canada, with his wife, children, his cat Loki, and far too many comic books. Follow Dante on Instagram @dantebilec.

Kurtis Rupé survived a career in financial services and now finds himself happily unemployed. He lived in Long Beach, Orange County, and the Bay Area of California before moving to Southern Arizona, with his partner and three dogs. His story "Ready to Take a Chance Again" was selected for *A Killing at the Copa: Crime Fiction Inspired by the Songs of Barry Manilow*, a soon-to-be-released anthology from White City Press. "Echoes of Lydia", a Speculative Fiction story, will also appear soon in the anthology "JR

Handley Presents: 'Face the Storm'" from Three Ravens Publishing. His poetry has been published in Chiron Review, Nerve Cowboy, and Pearl, and he recently won second place in a local limerick competition. When not writing, he takes Tai Chi classes, explores the beautiful Sonoran Desert, enjoys live music, and volunteers at his local nonprofit Friends of the Library bookstore.

M.J. McClymont is a writer of horror and fantasy fiction. He has written numerous short stories which have appeared in anthologies, magazines and websites since 2008. His work has been described as a mix of classic and contemporary, reminiscent of 70s and 80s horror fiction. M.J. McClymont's short story collection, *Dark Formations* was released early in 2024. You can find out more about his works here:

https://mmcclymont01.wixsite.com/mjmcclymont/books

E. Catherine Tobler's short fiction has appeared in *Clarkesworld, F&SF, Beneath Ceaseless Skies, Apex Magazine*, and others. Her short fiction has been a finalist for the Theodore Sturgeon Memorial Award and the Nebula Award. Her editorial work at *Shimmer* and *The Deadlands* has made her a finalist for the Hugo Award, the World Fantasy Award, and the Locus Award.

Erica Barnes likes pretending to live in a variety of worlds, whether by writing, reading, watching movies and television shows, or getting lost in her collection of video games. She has had short stories featured in Less Than Three Press' *Silver & Gold* anthology, as well as in Flame Tree Publishing's *Pirates & Ghosts Short Stories* anthology.

When she is not busy thinking of adventures she would like to go on, stories she wants to write, or treats she would like to bake, she can usually be found with her boyfriend, David, and her stepsons, Hunter and Bradley. She currently lives in West Virginia with her family, and hopes to one day publish a novel of her own. She would also like to give a shout out to her Christmas loving little sister, Brooke. If she does not, she may face a Santa sized wrath.

Justin Hunter is an author of 15 novels and is an award-winning screenwriter. He lives with his beautiful wife and five adopted boys in Missouri, USA. He can be contacted at justinhntr@yahoo.com for inquiries for available Horror/Comedy and Dark Drama film scripts and literary anthology invitations. He lives in a picturesque log home and every year people stop by and ask to take family Christmas photos in the yard. He tells them no.

Leon Peter Blanda is a writer and stand-up comedian. He cut his comedy teeth at dive bar open mics in New Orleans, Louisiana, and has featured for several of his heroes, including Bill Burr, Tom Segura, the Sklar Brothers, and more. In 2022, he released his debut novel, the genre-bending Western/adventure/horror, *High Moon*, followed by the coming-of-age novelette, *Dog Years*.
Leon Peter Blanda lives with his family, and a dog, near a swamp, in the Deep South.